\

Miss BOBBIN

By

Martyn Jones

ISBN: 978-1-914933-65-3

Illustrations by Matt Elliot

i2i Publishing. Manchester.
www.i2ipublishing.co.uk

Miss Bobbin

Mummy said to Bobbin "You had better get yourself ready my lovely girl."

"Yes," said Daddy, "You don't want to keep Grandad waiting."

"Oh!" cried Bobbin and put her favourite children's book down and ran to the stairs, stopped and asked "Mummy, what shall I wear?"

Mummy got up from her chair and shooing Bobbin upstairs said, "Up you go my girl and let's see," and chased her up the stairs. "I've packed your pyjamas, slippers and some fresh clothes for the morning."

"And don't forget your wellies," called Daddy.

Just a short time later they heard a car stop outside their house. The car door opening and then shutting, followed by footsteps slowly walking up their garden path towards the front door, then a cough from that someone at the door and a sudden sharp and loud rap-rap on the door.

Mummy, Daddy and Bobbin looked at each other wide-eyed.

"Who could that be?" asked Mummy.

Daddy looked at Bobbin and said "Well I don't know," shaking his head, puzzled.

Bobbin looked at both Mummy and Daddy and said very sensibly "I expect it's Grandad, we better open the door."

"Do you really think so Bobbin?" asked Mummy and Daddy together.

"Yes!" cried Bobbin, "Come on you two."

....

3

Daddy opened the front door and Bobbin looked out and there on the pathway was standing her Great Grandfather.

He and all her close family had always called her Bobbin; it was their pet name for her although her real name was Robyn which at times could be confusing, especially when at school. Great Grandfather would say to her "Great Grandfather is such a long name for you to call me, just call me Grandad. You Bobbin, me Grandad", much to both their amusement.

To Bobbin, her Grandad was a big man who looked even bigger in his winter storm coat and hat. He had a serious face that belied his gentle self. She could tell that her grandfather was very tall but her Daddy was even taller. But when Grandad looked at her it seemed to Bobbin as if he could see everything there was to know about her by just looking into her eyes, even what she was thinking. It was not until Grandad spoke to her in his strong, gentle voice she came to know how much he loved her and when he held her in his strong arms, how safe and comfortable, she felt.

"Are you ready Bobbin?" he asked, "We have to find young Oberon. His father can't find him anywhere and Titania's very worried. I'll tell you all about my woodland friends when we get in the car, come on Bobs."

Grandad lived in a cottage at the edge of the wild wood with her Great Grandmother Gigi. She always looked forward to seeing them both, especially as Gigi would have cooked her favourite 'Fruits of the Forest' cake for whenever she visited them.

Bobbin loved her Gigi's Forest fruit cake.

"So, Grandad, tell me who are Oberon and Titania?" she asked as Grandad was driving carefully through the narrow country lanes, with high hedges on both sides of the lane. If Bobbin looked carefully, she could just see cows and sheep in the fields through the hedges' winter branches.

"Titania is young Oberon's mummy. They are Red Deer, that's the biggest deer in this country of ours. Oberon's done this before, wandering off and frightening his mummy and daddy. I expect we'll soon find him though," said Grandad. He thought a few moments and spoke again. "His father will have a few words to say to him when we find him," and chuckled to himself.

"And what's his daddy's name?" Bobbin asked as Grandad turned off the lane and stopped at a secluded and picturesque woodland cottage.

Outside the cottage, she saw her Gigi was waiting for them at the garden gate, a worried look on her face. But when she saw Bobbin, her face lit up into a bright smile. She waved and called "Bobbin, come into the cottage and have a warm drink and a slice of my freshly baked forest cake before you and Grandad go off into the wood. I'm so worried about Oberon, he's wandered off somewhere again."

....

The gate at the bottom of the back garden led into the wild wood. The trees in the wood were very high and the ground beneath them covered with long grasses and small bushes. Bright winter sunlight shone through the treetops bathing the grass and shrubberies in pools of dappled sunshine.

Bobbin looked in wonder at the wood before her, hearing at first the sound of the wild wood's birdlife singing at the top of their voices, then seeing the birds for the first time, hopping from one branch to another and flying from one tree to another. There were no two birds that looked alike, some smaller than others, some prettier than others, each displaying different stripes and colours on their feathers and each singing a different song.

It seemed to Bobbin that the Wild Wood was full of life and song.

Grandad looked down at Bobbin and saw the wonder in her eyes as the wood and the animals that lived their lives there came to life, welcoming them both into their realm. Rabbits came out of their burrows, wood mice and shrews stood up on fallen tree branches to get a better view while the weasels and stoats ran round in circles chasing their tails in excitement and the wood pigeons cooed noisily in the tree tops.

"It's wonderful isn't it, Bobbin," said Grandad smiling.

"Oh Grandad," sighed the enchanted Bobbin "it's more than wonderful, it's beautiful and so much more."

"Bobbin, that's exactly how I felt the first time I saw this," Grandad replied and called a woodland greeting to the smaller folk of the wood. "But we must get on and speak to Alfred, he'll tell us where to find Lord Devon, come on. Do you want me to carry you?"

"No Grandad, I'm too old to be carried now" she laughed. "Who are Alfred and Lord Devon? I don't know them," asked Bobbin, looking up into her Grandad's eyes.

"My dear old friend Lord Devon is Oberon's father and Titania is his mother. Lord Devon is the Lord of the Wild Wood and the High Moor and Titania is his Lady". Grandad held out his hand which Bobbin took eagerly and was led down the path deeper into the wild wood.

"Oh yes, well Alfred is an owl, in fact a Wood Owl, the biggest owl in these woods. His flight is silent, so silent that none of the woodland folk know when he's coming or when he's gone. He just appears and then disappears. He knows everything that goes on in the wood and more. When I want to know something, I always ask my friend Alfred first and so will Lord Devon," said Grandad, his voice just above a whisper.

"Why are you whispering Grandad?" asked Bobbin.

Grandad smiled patiently, "We always whisper in the woods Bobbin, in case our loud voices frighten the small and timid animals that live here as well."

"Where does Alfred live?" said Bobbin, forgetting to whisper and said, "Oh sorry Grandad," again forgetting to whisper.

Grandad put a finger to his lips and said "Shh," gently.

Bobbin nodded her understanding and held a finger to her lips.

Grandad bent down and gathered Robyn in his arms, kissed her on the cheek and walked on placing his feet softly on the path, his footfall almost silent as Bobbin did her best to copy him.

"Well Alfred lives in a very, very old oak tree in the middle of the wood," he said quietly, "He will know where we can find Oberon. Let's speak to Alfred first then I'll tell you all about my dear friends the Red Deer and Lord Devon."

"Is it far Grandad?" said Robyn.

"We're almost there," he replied, frowned and stopped, turned round and looked back down the path. "I thought I heard you Bardon," Grandad said to a bearlike animal about the size of Bobbin's dog Manu, which was bumbling along the path trying to catch them up.

Bardon stopped and looked up at Bobbin and said to Grandad "Who's this? One of yours, is she?

"Yes, my friend, she's my Great Grandchild, you can call her Bobbin" and said to Bobbin, "This is Bardon the Badger and we have been friends since before your Mummy and Daddy were born."

Bardon snorted excitedly "I expect you're looking for Oberon, we all are. I'm going to Blade's house". Bardon looked up at Bobbin and said politely "Blade is my brother Miss Bobbin" and said to Grandad "He might have seen that scallywag Reynard who may know where Oberon is. I'll come and find you if that naughty fox knows anything" and turned off the path and trundled off into the undergrowth.

A short time later Bobbin and Grandad came upon a huge oak tree. It stood magnificent and majestic in the centre of a small meadow surrounded by shimmering silver birch and ash trees. The oak was dark and a little foreboding against the threatening winter sky, its trunk notched and gnarled, the branches thick and long, giving many places for the small animals of the forest to hide and nest. Alfred lived in the bole of the oak, high up giving him shelter from the winter rain and snow, with excellent views of the surrounding woodland. He had seen Grandad and Bobbin coming from the edge of the wood and dropped silently down to a lower branch to greet them.

"Good morning, Alfred," said Grandad. "How are you and all your family keeping?"

Bobbin looked up in amazement, for perched on a lower branch of the oak tree was an owl almost as big as she was and quite frightening to see. She looked in awe at the bird thanking her lucky stars she was with Grandad.

Grandad felt her stir and said quietly "Don't be afraid Bobbin, Alfred is our friend."

Alfred looked at Bobbin and said gently "Did I startle you, Miss Bobbin? Your Grandad here has told me all about you. All of us Wild Wood folk have been waiting to meet you. Ever since you were born, I fly over your house at night making sure you and your Mummy and Daddy are sleeping safely."

Grandad looked at Bobbin and said "What do you say to that Bobbin?" Bobbin took a deep breath, swallowed and said seriously looking at the owl "Thank you very much Alfred. I shall tell my Mummy and Daddy what you said."

The owl gazed at Bobbin for a while and then said "Perhaps one day child, but not yet" and slowly nodded his head twice and turned to Grandad. "Please bring Miss Bobbin to see me when you can, I'd like to speak with her some more."

"I will Alfred, thank you. But more urgently we must find young Oberon, he seems to have wandered off somewhere again," said Grandad.

"Yes, so I have heard. I think the first place to look should be the high moorland. When the light begins to dim, I will fly over there and let you and Lord Devon know where he is," said Alfred. "You Grandad, go and find Lord Devon and the Lady Titania. I expect you'll find them at the Secret Lake. Tell them not to worry, my friends and I will find Oberon. Goodbye for now Miss

Bobbin" and opened his wings and flew silently back to his owl home high up in the old oak.

Bobbin regarded her Great Grandfather seriously and said in a quiet even voice "I am thunderstruck. I didn't know you were friends with so many of the Wild Wood folk Grandad. Can I tell Mummy and Daddy when they pick me up tomorrow?"

Grandad smiled, then pursed his lips in thought. "I wouldn't tell Mummy and Daddy just yet, I'll tell you when the time is right. Alfred and I have been friends for so many years, apart from that scallywag Reynard the Fox and he only speaks when he wants something. He needs to learn some manners. Come on Bobbin let's go and find Lord Devon," said Grandad and rubbed his shoulder.

"Where will we find Lord Devon?" said Bobbin and took Grandad's hand as they both walked off towards the Secret Lake.

Alfred the owl called down from his home high in the old oak "That's the second time you have rubbed your shoulder Grandad. I will think on it, some balm should be the answer."

....

The Secret Lake was hidden away, almost but not quite at the far side of the wood. It was the home of Hernshaw the Heron, Flash the Kingfisher, several duck families, water birds such as the moorhens and their cousins the coots. Also, a family of geese would visit for a few weeks then fly off somewhere towards the northlands in the early spring.

It was here that Grandad and Bobbin saw Lord Devon and the Lady Titania across the lake. Both Red Deer raised their heads in respectful greeting to Grandad and gazed in interest at Bobbin and began to walk, delicately placing their footsteps with care and consideration round the edge of the lake towards their friend.

Grandad and Bobbin followed the lakeside to meet his friends, saying to Bobbin "Don't be afraid Bobbin my friends know about you and are eager to meet you. Just be yourself."

"I'll try Grandad," said the nervous Bobbin and looked at the tall, powerfully built stag with a pair of great antlers crowning his head. Bobbin understood why he was called The Lord Devon, for he had a regal and noble air, his very presence radiating his power and authority.

Bobbin knew instinctively it would be more respectful to wait to be addressed by the giant stag before trying to speak to him and so waited.

"Good morning, Grandad," said the stag, "My Lady Titania and I are so very pleased to have your company this day. You may have heard our son Oberon has wandered off again," and looked at Bobbin, the bottomless dark pools of his eyes gazing at her in interest."

"Yes, my Lord, Bobbin and I have spoken to Alfred and Bardon. He'll be found soon. Alfred thinks he may have wandered onto the High Moor and will fly up there this evening," said Grandad, matching Lord Devon's dignity.

"Thank you, Grandad, my dear old friend. Would you please introduce us to Bobbin? It's the first time we have met her," said the stag and turned to Titania who was standing quietly at her Lord's side smiling at Bobbin.

"Of course, Lord Devon, Lady Titania, this is my beloved Great Grand Daughter Robyn, known to us who love her as Bobbin," spoke Grandad proudly and rubbed his shoulder once more.

The Lord Devon bowed his great crown of antlers to Bobbin as the Lady Titania stepped past her Lord and said gently "Bobbin, how lovely to meet you at last, I do hope we will see you here often." Her face was happy, her eyes sad with the worry of Oberon, her tears still wet on her cheeks.

Bobbin looked at Lady Titania for a while, then took a deep breath and spoke quietly with a knowledge she did not know she had. "Don't be sad Lady Titania, something tells me that Oberon is safe and will be home tomorrow morning." Taking a handkerchief from her pocket, she stepped up to the Lady Titania and gently wiped away the tears from her cheeks.

....

Alfred the owl had circled the High Moor several times in the moonlight not seeing anything of Oberon. Then suddenly he flew over a small cluster of rhododendron bushes and there saw the young Red Deer drinking from a fast-flowing upland stream almost hidden by the bushes.

The evening was getting darker, clouds beginning to dull the moonlight and luckily if it were not for the fading moonlight, he might not have seen the deer.

He swooped low over Oberon who looked up startled at the owl's sudden appearance, no flap of wings, no draft of air betraying Alfred's arrival as he alighted on a nearby wind-twisted, weather-beaten rowan tree and stared at the young deer in displeasure.

....

Grandad and Bobbin arrived back at the woodland cottage just as it was getting dark. Gigi opened the kitchen door, the light behind her giving a warm bright halo around her. She picked up the tired Bobbin in her arms and sat her near the log fire, gently eased her out of her coat and slipped off her wellington boots.

"You sit there for a moment Bobbin and I'll get you a bowl of my countryside stew," said Gigi. "Are you ready for some Grandad? she asked.

"Yes, please Gigi, I'm feeling hungry and cold." He sat himself in the armchair opposite Bobbin and holding out his hands to the fire said "When you've finished the stew, Gigi will put you to bed and I'll come up and read you a story about the fairies that live in the wood."

"When will Mummy and Daddy take me home Grandad?" she asked, a look of longing in her eyes.

"They'll be here tomorrow afternoon and after they have their Sunday dinner, they'll take you home," answered Gigi.

Bobbin took another spoonful of her stew, wiped her mouth with a napkin and said "The stew is lovely Gigi, can I have some more please?"

Grandad and Gigi both laughed and said together "Of course our lovely girl."

Then a more serious Bobbin asked Grandad "Are there really fairies in the Wild Wood Grandad?"

Grandad looked at her equally as seriously "Yes Bobbin, but you have to believe in them before they show themselves to you."

....

"Oh, Alfred it's you. I've lost my way home in this dim evening light. Which way is it?" said Oberon pleased to see his friend the owl.

"Yes Oberon, you have wandered off again haven't you?" Alfred said seriously to his Lord's young son.

Oberon lowered his head in shame and answered in a quiet voice "Yes, I have Alfred. Is my father angry with me?"

Alfred thought for a moment looking at the young Oberon kindly. He had known the child, then the boy and now the young and growing Oberon, since Devon and Titania had first shown their new born to the Wild Wood folk, The Lord Devon announcing to all proudly "This is our son Oberon. One day he will become your Lord Oberon. And so, I ask you all to take care of him in his young years, until the time comes when he will take care of you as he takes the Mantle of Hope from me someday."

....

Grandad came down the cottage stairs carrying the book of fairies and said to Gigi "Our Bobbin is sound a sleep. I opened the first page of my book, looked up and there she was fallen asleep." He smiled at the memory as his phone rang.

"How's Bobbin Grandad?" It was her Daddy. "Is she missing us?"

Grandad smiled to himself and whispered to Gigi "It's James with Sophie no doubt listening in."

"Well," said Grandad, "Bobbin asked about you both once between mouthfuls of Gigi's stew. Then seems to have forgotten you." He laughed down the phone. "She's sound a sleep now, we shouldn't wake her James."

"No, no Grandad we are just checking everything's alright. We'll be home tomorrow afternoon and we'll stop by and pick Bobbin up then," said James.

Gigi called over Grandad's shoulder "Are you and Sophie having a nice time James?"

"We are Gigi but missing our Bobbin though," replied James.

"There'll be dinner waiting for you both when you arrive," said Gigi.

"We'll look forward to that," called Sophie.

....

"Oberon!" Alfred almost shouted. It was most unlike him and continued sternly but quieter this time, "Your father the Lord Devon is very concerned about you boy. He will be angry, but only after he sees you are safe home again."

Oberon looked up at where the owl was perched and said "I've been very silly haven't I Alfred?"

"Your mother!" interrupted Alfred "The Lady Titania is in tears all the time. She is so upset about you she is beside herself," he said angrily, which was unusual for Alfred as he too loved the young Oberon in his own owl way.

"Oh, dear Alfred, I had better go home straight away," said the now shocked Oberon. Only now was he beginning to realise the seriousness of what he had done.

The owl tutted and shook his head "Not now young Oberon, you must stay here and rest until morning. You may injure yourself in the darkness," said Alfred more gently this time, his anger almost gone. "And don't worry, I will speak to your father and tell him how ashamed and worried you are about your parents."

"Thank you, Alfred," said the tearful Oberon. "It is so comforting to know you are my friend. One day you will be my even closer friend, so my father tells me."

Alfred smiled and leaned down and gently touched Oberon's shoulder with his wing tip "So I want you now to settle down and rest through the time of darkness. Make no noise, be silent while I go and see Moonbeam the Otter. I saw him earlier when I flew over the wide river, he was fishing for river oysters, a very tasty meal as I recall. Well anyway," he said fluffing up his feathers. "I'll tell him to go to your parents and tell them you are well and will be at the Secret Lake in the morning time." He looked at Oberon more seriously, took his wing tip off Oberon's shoulder and pointed it at him and said "You young Oberon are to stay here and take care of yourself through the night. I shall return at dawn and show you the way home." He opened his great wings and flew off silently towards the moon.

Bobbin was eating her breakfast in Gigi's kitchen when her Great Grandmother said looking through the window into the back garden "Grandad is speaking to a Little Owl, one of Alfred's cousins. Let's hope it's news of Oberon."

Looking over the sink and through the kitchen window Bobbin saw the Little Owl fly off back into the Wild Wood. Then the door opened and in stepped Grandad and asked Gigi if the tea was still hot in the teapot.

"Should be Grandad or maybe not," she answered and winked at Bobbin.

Grandad sat across the table from Bobbin and poured a small amount of milk into a large chipped and stained cup that had the name Grandad printed on it. "Just in case any visitor doesn't know it is my cup," he would always tell family and friends who visited the cottage.

Bobbin watched as her Grandad leaned across the table, pick up the teapot, sit back in his chair and pour tea into his cup filling it almost to the brim.

"Well, what did the Little Owl have to say Grandad?" Gigi asked looking at the cup in Grandad's hand.

"Oh yes, Burnet the Little Owl told me...," said Grandad looking at his cup of tea, "Alfred found Oberon last night and he's on his way from the High Moor to the Secret Lake now." Grandad looked over the table at Bobbin and seeing she had finished her breakfast said "Get your coat and wellies on Bobbin, we're off to see Oberon's homecoming," and putting the cup to his lips took a big sip of tea.

"Uhh!" said Grandad, putting his cup back on the table "This tea's cold Gigi."

Bobbin and Gigi laughed loudly at Grandad and said together, "We thought it might be Grandad."

The large and small animals of the Wild Wood lined the pathway as Oberon approached the Secret Lake.

Everyone knew how naughty Oberon had been and they all wanted to see him and wish him luck.

Bardon the Badger was there with his brother Blade both calling to him how happy they were to see him safe and well.

Moonbeam the Otter whistled a greeting to him from the middle of the Secret Lake and turned on his back and swam backwards waving at him.

The trees at the sides of the path were full of woodland birds singing their greetings, each to a different tune. The rabbits were happily hopping along behind Oberon.

Wood mice and shrews were running alongside, jumping from one fallen log to another, while the weasels and stoats danced together in front of the now nervous Oberon. The pigeons could be heard cooing loudly in the treetops.

Oberon had greeted all the Wild Wood folk with his nervous smile as he stepped out of the wood and onto the shore of the Secret Lake.

Across the lake standing tall and proud, was The Lord Devon, his head held high, his crown of antlers announcing to all watching Oberon's homecoming, that their Lord Devon was the Lord of their Wild Wood, Lord of the surrounding High Moor and Lord of all the countryside folk that lived there.

Oberon stopped and looking across the lake saw his mother, who was eagerly smiling her love to him. He looked at his father and hesitated, took a deep breath, gathered his courage round him, looked at his father again and stepped on towards his parents.

The Lord Devon's face remained unsmiling and impassive, deliberately giving no clue as to what he was thinking.

Robyn and Grandad stood in respectful silence behind The Lord Devon and his Lady Titania holding each other's hand. Then Bobbin, not being able to contain herself any longer whispered to Grandad "What will Lord Devon do to poor Oberon? Do you think he will tell him off Grandad?

"I should think so Bobbin. He deserves to be Told Off for putting his parents through all this worry," said Grandad briefly. "Remember how tearful the Lady Titania was yesterday."

Robyn nodded in agreement, "Yes Grandad, but I'm not sure if I want Oberon Told Off or not. Look at him, he looks so nervous."

Alfred the owl was sat on a low branch that reached out over the lake close to where Grandad and Bobbin were standing and had heard them speak to each other. He coughed just loud enough to get their attention and spoke just above a whisper,

"Miss Bobbin, I understand your thoughts, they do you justice and I am impressed my child. But also know the Lord Devon loves his son Oberon just as much as Lady Titania. However, you must remember it is his duty to see his son knows his faults and learns by his mistakes. Oberon will be the Lord of all this someday," said Alfred sweeping his wing round the lake and pointing up over the trees to the high moor "and must be shown the consequences of his thoughtless actions." The owl tucked his wing away to his side and regarded Bobbin silently.

"That's right Bobbin," agreed Grandad "all the Wild Wood folk have been awake through the dark night looking for and worrying about Oberon," and shifted his feet and rubbed his shoulder again.

"Umm" said a thoughtful Bobbin still unsure how she really felt "I don't want him to be Told Off though. Look at him. He's so handsome."

Grandad and Alfred looked at each other and smiled.

Reynard the Fox had been sitting behind the tree listening and ran forward and sat under the branch Alfred was sitting on.

Bobbin was startled by the fox's sudden appearance and quickly took hold of Grandad's hand.

Grandad spoke gently to the fox, "Reynard my friend, you know better then to frighten children. I know you didn't mean to, but please be more careful though." and wagged a finger at him.

Reynard dropped his head down almost to the ground in apology and looked up at Bobbin with soulful eyes and quickly said:

"Sorry Miss Bobbin, I shall never behave again like that in your presence."

"How totally unconvincing you scallywag! said Alfred angrily. "Behave yourself Reynard or you'll have me to answer to."

Again, Reynard dropped his head all the way to the ground this time. Alfred had called him by his name which he only did when he was really angry. The naughty fox much preferred to be called scallywag when he was caught doing anything wrong by Alfred and said quietly "I truly apologise Alfred, how thoughtless of me."

"Then stand up straight and listen to me," and turned to Grandad and said "I see you have your shoulder pain again. Let me see if I can find you some herbs. They are scarce this time of year, but I think I know where to find them."

....

Oberon had almost reached the far side of the lake where his mother and father waited, knowing he must show dignity and take responsibility for his thoughtlessness, especially to his father. He stood up straighter, held his head higher and walked with quiet confidence the last few yards to where The Lord Devon, his father and The Lady Titania, his mother waited.

The large and small Wild Wood folk lining the path fell silent.

Bardon the Badger with his brother Blade found a place in the high grass where they could be unseen and wait to see what was going to happen.

Moonbeam the Otter swam to the water's edge and hid among the remains of the summer's Bull Rushes, his nose and eyes just visible among reeds.

The birds fell silent, and even the pigeons stopped their cooing.

The rabbits and forest mice and shrews stopped their leaping and waited, while the stoats and weasels suddenly disappeared unable to take the strain of not knowing what was going to happen.

The Wild Wood and Secret Lake fell silent as everyone held their breath, all the woodland folk wondering if Oberon was going to be Told Off.

The Lord Devon stepped forward having first asked his Lady Titania to remain where she was, saying tenderly to her "Let me meet our son first and I will bring him to you, my love."

"I will my Lord," said Lady Titania quietly.

Oberon drew closer to his father feeling himself getting more nervous with each step he took. Then he remembered the words spoken by his father when he had grown from a fawn into a young stag, "Oberon my son, never show fear or nervousness, only show dignity and respect."

The thought of his father's advice calmed Oberon's nerves and so he stepped on looking his father respectfully in the eyes.

Bobbin looked up at her Great Grand Father and squeezed his hand. Grandad looked down at his beloved Bobbin and smiled.

Bobbin put a finger up to her lips and very quietly said "Shh".

Grandad nodded.

The two Red Deer came together and Oberon looked up at his father.

The Lord Devon looked down on his son with love shining from his eyes.

The birds and the animals of the Wild Wood now hidden in the trees and the surrounding wood all held their breaths once more, as Oberon took a deep breath and dropping his head in respect said in a firm voice, that was just loud enough for the animals of the Wild Wood to hear.

"Father, I am so sorry and ashamed that I have once again worried you and my mother so much." He then lifted his head and looked his father in the eyes again saying, "It will not happen again father, I have been taught a lesson and Alfred has shown me how thoughtless I have been."

There was a rising murmur heard coming from the surrounding woodland as the birds and animals began to discuss Oberon's apology.

The Lord Devon quickly brought his head upright and gave his antlers a powerful shake.

All the woodland folk fell silent again.

Reynard the Fox sniggered and Alfred the owl flapped a wing. The naughty fox too fell silent looking at Alfred.

The Lord Devon spoke with quiet dignity, "Oberon my son, it is wonderful to have you home safely in the Wild Wood again. We have been worried." It came from his heart and he laid his head gently over Oberon's shoulder.

Oberon felt his tears flow from his eyes and laid his head against his father's shoulder. The Lord Devon lifted his head and said "Come and greet your mother," and stepped aside as mother and son ran to each other.

The excited sound of cheering and the flapping of wings was clearly heard from the treetops and woodland, with loud whistles coming from the lake.

Bobbin looked up at Grandad almost shouting in her happiness, "I am so happy, how wonderful Grandad!"

"Yes, it is Bobbin, Wonderful is the right word," said Grandad smiling down at Bobbin.

"Well!" said the disappointed fox, "That's not what I would call being Told Off!"

"Oh, do be quiet you scallywag!" said Alfred angrily. "I want you to go to the hidden bank by the tallest pine tree in the wood where the Columbine grows. You know it don't you Reynard?"

"Yes Alfred," said the Fox eagerly, knowing it was the second time this day he had upset the owl and the second time the owl had called him by his name. "Oh dear," he said to himself.

"Among the Columbine you will find plenty of Wood Anemones. Pick a bunch and take them to Grandad's cottage. Leave them at the kitchen door and be quick about it, you scallywag."

The fox ran off smiling to himself. He knew Alfred loved him really. It was just that he seemed to displease him so much and he did not know why. Reynard the Fox shook his head in puzzlement and ran on.

"Gently simmer the herbs down to a paste Grandad. Let it cool and then get Gigi to rub it into your shoulder," said Alfred looking over at the three Red Deer walking off slowly together into the Wild Wood side by side, young Oberon between his parents, each touching each other's shoulder.

Bobbin sighed at the picture of happiness.

Grandad said "Come on Bobbin, let's get back to the cottage. Your Mummy and Daddy will be there soon."

They both heard Alfred the owl call as he flew silently back to his oak tree, "Come back and see me soon Miss Bobbin."

The Rescue of Reynard the Fox

Hernshaw the Heron stood silent and still at the water's edge looking across the Secret Lake to where Moonbeam the Otter was lazing in the afternoon sunshine. He stood so still that his different shades of grey and ivory feathers and the even lighter grey of his mantle, which draped over his shoulders and down his back, made Hernshaw almost invisible. Indeed, when he was among the tall reeds and rushes standing straight, his head held high it was mostly impossible to see him.

Not so for Moonbeam the Otter though. He had seen Hernshaw from all the way across the lake and whistled softly to him "I can see you Hernshaw, you can't hide from me," and rolled over playfully and waved his paws at his friend.

"Do be quiet Moonbeam," croaked the exasperated Heron, "I'm looking for my breakfast," and continued his gaze onto the shallow water gently lapping against the reeds.

"Ah Hernshaw, there you are. I can never see you when you stand so still like that," shouted Flash the Kingfisher and alighted on a tall reed just above Hernshaw's head.

"Oh, fiddlesticks!" cried Hernshaw "What is it now Flash, I'm trying, but obviously not very successfully, to have my breakfast."

"You need to get up earlier then," teased Moonbeam from across the lake. "The sun is up and I had my breakfast some time ago." On the breeze that rippled the water Hernshaw and Flash heard the Otter's laughter.

The fairies that make the wind blow across the lake all took a deep breath and blew over the water causing the reeds to bend, making Flash open his wings to steady himself exposing his brilliant iridescent blue back feathers.

These are so eye-catching and normally the only thing to be seen as he flies across the lake almost touching the water.

"Oops," said Flash.

"Steady there," said Hernshaw. "You had better tell me what's on your mind Flash before the wind fairies blow you out of the reeds." He smiled patiently.

"Well," answered Flash, "I've been fishing at the big river on the High Moor and have just seen Reynard the Fox. I think he's been injured. He's limping quite badly and can't get back to the Wild Wood." The Kingfisher flapped his wings to show how very important he thought it all was.

Hernshaw listened quietly to what Flash had to say and thought for a moment, then looked over at Moonbeam the Otter and called out to him, "Moonbeam! Come over here, quickly."

Moonbeam immediately lifted his head sensing the urgency in Hernshaw's voice, stood and dived gracefully into the lake leaving hardly a ripple, just a small ring of bubbles that glinted in the sunlight, and swam fast towards Hernshaw and Flash, just his eyes and nose visible above the water.

Flash snorted angrily, "I'm not speaking to Moonbeam he keeps eating my fish!" and in a brilliant flash of bright blue he flew off.

"And mine," called Hernshaw after his friend the Kingfisher. "It's what Otters do."

"What's all the excitement about Hernshaw? asked Moonbeam.

"Flash has told me that Reynard the Fox is on the High Moor, he has injured himself. He can't get back to the Wild Wood," gasped Hernshaw, feeling quite tearful on hearing of Reynard's predicament.

Moonbeam remained silent looking into the watery eyes of his friend. "Ok," he said at last knowing what he must do, "I'll go and speak to Alfred, he'll know what must be done. I expect he'll have a word with Grandad." Moonbeam slipped away again into the lake and swam even faster this time back to the other side, then sprang from the lake and disappeared into the Wild Wood.

....

Burnet the Little Owl heard Alfred's call from deep in the Wild Wood. He lived in an ancient quarry, once a busy noisy place as dozens of men dug out the rocks to build their homes. Now a hundred years later, it was a quiet and hidden place with small, stunted trees and bushes giving an abandoned feeling to visitors. In the summertime, the walls and discarded rocks of the quarry would be covered with wildflowers and small delicate orchids, which would hide themselves in the secret places. Now in the winter, the quarry was covered in mosses and fallen leaves, its trees and bushes now bare of leaves, while all the plants and animals that lived there waited for springtime.

Burnet's home was in a deep hidden ledge in the quarry wall where he had been hatched from his mother's egg. When he had grown, Alfred, his Great Cousin, had given him the very important title of the Wild Wood's Messenger.

Burnet was proud to be known as the Messenger and loved his cousin Alfred.

Burnet flew at speed through the wood, gliding round large trees and winging fast in the more open glades and small meadows and on reaching Alfred's oak he landed on a branch just below the Wood Owl's home and waited.

....

"Ah Burnet, thank you for coming over so quickly," said Alfred silently appearing at his doorstep "How are you and your family keeping? You look very well I must say. Your feathers are shining."

"Thank you, Great Cousin Alfred," said Burnet and dropped his head down to his chest and blushed. Alfred always made Little Burnet blush with his kind words for Burnet took his position of the Wild Wood's Messenger very seriously.

"Now Burnet, I have an important message for you to deliver to Grandad or Gigi, it doesn't matter which one." He ruffled his feathers and flapped his wings once thinking of the message he was to give to his young messenger.

"This must be serious Great Cousin Alfred," said the Little Owl, suddenly feeling the responsibility of having to deliver an important message to Grandad or Gigi.

"Yes, it is young Burnet. Now you shoosh and let me think on what I'm about to say to you," said Alfred, his words kind and gentle to his cousin.

"Yes of course Alfred, I so sorry to interrupt you when you're thinking," gasped Burnet, feeling foolish. "I'll let you...."

"Burnet!" interrupted Alfred "Shoosh," he said and smiled at Burnet who smiled shyly back and nodded his head.

Alfred, having thought carefully, said quietly to Burnet, speaking slowly so the young Little Owl would hopefully remember all of his message. "Your message is Burnet, that Reynard the scallywag is on the High Moor close to where Oberon waited for me to guide him back to the Secret Lake. Do you remember?" he asked.

Burnet nodded.

"We think he is injured and needs help to get back to the Wild Wood. Would Grandad help?" Alfred thought some more and added "This evening, tell Grandad, I'll fly to Miss Bobbin's house and ask her to get her Mummy and Daddy to drive her to Grandad's cottage first thing in the morning. Can you remember all that Burnet?"

"Yes Alfred," replied the Little Owl eagerly.

"Well off you go then. Be careful, don't fly too fast," called Alfred as Burnet opened his wings and flew off silently.

Alfred huffed and puffed saying to Burnet's back as he flew away "I was going to say Burnet I will find Blade the Badger and ask him to go up to the High Moor and keep Reynard company through the night." He then smiled, shrugged his shoulders saying to himself "Well never mind," and flew off towards Blade's home.

....

Burnet the Little Owl landed on the gate post at the back garden of Grandad's cottage. The light was fading as the day slowly turned into night. There was already a light shining through the cottage kitchen window as Burnet remembered he must be patient for sooner or later either Grandad or Gigi would look out of their window and see him, and so settled comfortably and waited.

....

In the dim moody twilight, Alfred the Owl arrived at the very edge of the Wild Wood, almost where the wood ended and the moor began. For there on a bank, under an oak tree, even older than the oak where Alfred lived, was hidden among brambles and bracken was an entrance of a short tunnel that led to where Blade had his comfortable home. His warm and snug chamber was lined with dry leaves and sweet-smelling grasses he had collected in the autumn before the winter frosts and rain had a chance to rot them.

Alfred dropped onto the ground by Blade's set and called softly down the tunnel "Blade, Blade are you awake yet? It's almost dark, you should be up and out of your bed by now," he teased knowing his friend was always irritable when first waking up.

Blade appeared at the entrance of his set "Of course I'm up Alfred, I've been up for ages thank you. I'm just about to have my breakfast. Come on in and join me, I have porridge and honey bubbling away on the stove."

"Tut tut!" said Alfred impatiently "You don't have time for porridge and honey now. Take the pot off your stove and listen to me please old friend."

Blade was a sensible and learned old badger, twice as wise as his brother Bardon who Alfred knew he loved dearly. In the depth of wintertime when the snow was deep on the wood's frozen ground, he would have his stove burning brightly in his chamber and cook his favourite meals, read ancient books of the old woodland folk who had lived their lives in the Wild Wood countless seasons ago. *For knowing the past was to prepare for the future,* he would always say to himself.

"This sounds serious Alfred. What an earth is the matter old friend?" asked Blade, now worried. "Is it Oberon again worrying the life out of us all?"

"Heavens no Blade, it's that scallywag Reynard. Flash the Kingfisher thinks he's hurt and can't get home to the Wild Wood," replied Alfred. "I've sent Burnet to alert Grandad and I'm off to see Miss Bobbin. I've a feeling we're going to need their help," and flapped his wings showing how concerned he was.

Blade nodded "What can I do to help!" and sat up on his hind legs, his front powerful paws held high displaying he was ready to do anything for Alfred.

"Well, I think Blade," said Alfred, thinking over the problem, "I want you to find Reynard and stay with him throughout the dark night just in case those High Moor stoats and weasels gang up on him. They don't like us Wild Wood folk!" He thought some more, "Oh yes, first find The Lord Devon and tell him we may just need him to help," said Alfred, thinking some more and wondering if he had forgotten anything.

"I will Alfred, let me eat my porridge and honey first and I'll be off my friend," said Blade, who turned and rushed off down the tunnel to his chamber.

"Thank you Blade, I'm off to Miss Bobbin's house and tell her to tell her mummy and daddy she's wanted at

Grandad's cottage the first thing in the morning." shouted Alfred at the rapidly disappearing Blade.

....

Burnet had been waiting some while on the cottage garden's gate post when he suddenly saw Gigi gazing out of the window at him. Relieved his wait was over, Burnet flapped his wings twice, signalling his message was urgent.

"Grandad," called Gigi, "Burnet the Little Owl is at the gate post and wanting to speak to you urgently," and went to their front room as Grandad put down his book and began to climb out of his comfortable armchair. "Better put your hat and coat on, it looks cold out there," said Gigi, helping Grandad up.

"Thanks Gigi, I was just about to drop off then. What time is it?" said Grandad, shaking himself and bending his knees.

"It's nearly 8 o'clock. Whatever could it be," answered Gigi. "Don't stay out there too long now, you'll catch one of your colds again."

In the kitchen, Grandad put on his jacket and cap and opened the kitchen door "Phew! You're right Gigi it's freezing out here." He closed the door and walked down the garden path to his little friend Burnet.

"Hello Grandad, I'm sorry to disturb you this time of the evening, especially now it's so cold and dark. Oh, how are you and Gigi keeping? My friends are always asking about you," spoke the Little Owl very politely.

Grandad pulled his jacket tighter round himself and turned up the collar. "We're well thank you Burnet, but I think you have an urgent message for me. Don't you?"

Grandad was amused. The Wild Wood folk were so very polite it took ages for them to come to the point.

Burnet was startled when Grandad reminded him of his message. "Oh yes, I nearly forgot Grandad. Alfred would be so very angry," he said and looked at Grandad waiting for his sympathy and his usual kind words.

"Yes," said Grandad, "and your message Burnet?" He smiled.

"Oh yes," and paused recalling Alfred's message "Reynard the Fox has hurt his leg on the High Moor and cannot get home. My Great Cousin Alfred has asked Blade the Badger to go and stay with Reynard while it's dark." He stopped and thought for a moment remembering the whole message. "Oh yes Grandad, Alfred asks that you and Miss Bobbin go to the High moor in the morning and help get Reynard back to the Wild Wood." He stopped again wondering if he had remembered all Alfred's message "Oh yes, I almost forgot Grandad, silly me.."

"Yes, yes Burnet, get on with it," said the laughing Grandad.

"Oh yes, sorry Grandad. Alfred also sent Blade to find the Lord Devon to help as well. Great cousin Alfred was then going to fly over to Miss Bobbin's house and ask her to tell her mummy and daddy to take her to Grandad's first thing in the morning." Burnet nodded his head relieved he had delivered all Alfred's message and gazed at Grandad pleased with himself.

"Well done young Burnet, I'll tell Alfred you remembered all of his message and what a good messenger you are," said Grandad.

"Tell Alfred, Bobbin and I will be on the High Moor tomorrow morning, first thing. Off you go now."

Burnet the Little Owl puffed up his feathers in delight and flew off back into the dark Wild Wood.

....

"You should be in bed my girl," said Daddy looking up from his laptop. "It's quite dark out there now," and looked over at Bobbin's Mummy and raised his eyebrows.

"Yes, Bobbin up the stairs you go my lovely girl," she said, and put down her knitting and stood up and held out her arms to Bobbin.

"Get yourself into bed Bobbin and I'll come up and tuck you in," called Daddy, closing down his laptop for the night.

In her bedroom, Bobbin kissed and said goodnight to her Mummy and climbed into her bed. But as soon as Mummy had left the room there was a gentle tapping on the window. Bobbin looked across her bedroom at the window and immediately saw Alfred perched outside the window. She jumped out of bed and ran to the window and pulled it open, pleased to see her friend again.

"I am so very sorry to disturb you Miss Bobbin, I know it's late and you should be asleep," whispered Alfred, concerned he might alarm Bobbin's Mummy and Daddy.

"You don't need to whisper Alfred I've told Mummy and Daddy all about you," said the smiling Bobbin. "But I'm not sure they really believe me."

"Well yes, Miss Bobbin thank you but I didn't want to frighten your Mummy and Daddy. The thing is, you and Grandad are needed on the High Moor first thing in the morning. Reynard has hurt himself and needs to get home. My cousin the young Burnet is telling Grandad now and so would you ask your Mummy and Daddy to take you to Grandad's as soon as it gets light? said Alfred urgently and almost breathless after his flight from the Wild Wood, just as her bedroom door opened and in stepped her Daddy.

"Who on earth are you speaking to Bobbin? And close that window it's too cold outside for open windows my girl," said daddy unaware of Alfred's presence on the window sill.

"Oh!" said Bobbin and looked at her daddy and then back at Alfred who had disappeared. He had silently flown off back to the Wild Wood.

Bobbin closed her window wondering what she was going to say to her daddy, made up her mind and said "I've been speaking to Alfred. He tells me.............." Her daddy's mobile phone rang in his pocket.

Daddy answered his phone "Oh hello Grandad," and frowned, "Is everything alright, is Gigi ok?" wondering if there was a problem with his grandparents.

"Stop worrying my boy, we are both ok." Grandad paused and heard his grandson's sigh of relief. "It's just that I want you to drive Bobbin over to me first thing in the morning. She can help me with something that needs doing in the woods. Is that ok," asked Grandad crossing his fingers.

"I can drop her off on my way to work Grandad and pick her up again on my way home," said Daddy. "What's she helping you with?" he asked intrigued.

"Oh dear," thought Grandad, *"I should have had my answer ready"* and was just about to find an answer when Bobbin said,

"Grandad wants me to help him take some orphaned bunnies back to the cottage," said Bobbin and crossed her fingers behind her back to ask for forgiveness for the white fib she had just told.

Daddy looked at Bobbin and frowned again. "How did you know that?"

There was a second's silence in the room then Grandad said "Telepathy!" and stifled a laugh.

"Yes!" said the relieved Bobbin, "that's it Daddy, telepathy. I couldn't think of the word Grandad."

"That's it then. I'll see you in the morning Bobbin. Goodnight, sleep tight," said the amused Grandad.

Daddy stood at the bottom of Bobbin's bed and scratched his head. "Into bed with you my girl, you're up early in the morning," and was just about to close Bobbin's bedroom door when he asked, "Oh, by the way, who's Alfred?"

"Alfred? Alfred who?" and jumped into her bed and pulled the cover over her head so Daddy could not hear her giggling.

....

Meanwhile...

Blade found Reynard as the moon appeared through a sudden break in the clouds, throwing a pale eerie light fleetingly as the clouds closed again and the night became dark once more.

But Blade had spotted Reynard as he limped painfully along the river bank and called softly to him "Reynard, you were told to stay still and quiet. Wait there I'm coming."

"Sorry Blade, it was those horrible High Moor stoats and weasels. I could hear them talking about me," he said, relieved to see Blade come to his rescue. "They were going to wait until the morning light, then ask the Crows to find my hiding place. I thought I had better try and get back to the Wild Wood, but my foot is hurting so much."

"I'm not worried about those High Moor stoats and weasels but the crows are not nice," said Blade. "Let's hide under this mulberry bush and wait until Grandad gets here," and heard Reynard sigh with relief.

"Grandad! How wonderful, I'm beginning to think everything's going to be alright. And I am so pleased that you are here as well Blade," Reynard said as a tear trickled down his red cheek.

"And I and my son Oberon are here also you scallywag, to guard you through the night," said the Lord Devon and his son Oberon as they stepped out of the darkness, Devon's majestic crown of antlers displaying his power against the cloudy night sky.

"My Lord Devon!" gasped Reynard. "Oberon! How you have grown. How can I ever repay you my Lord?"

"I'll think of something Reynard," replied Lord Devon and winked at Blade who nodded back knowingly to his Lord.

....

Daddy stopped his car outside Grandad's cottage and Bobbin leaned over the front seat and kissed her father, jumped out of the car and ran to Gigi's open arms.

"Let's get inside Bobbin before we both freeze solid," laughed her Great Grandmother.

In the kitchen Grandad was sat at the table eating his breakfast of porridge with his hat on, his scarf and coat draped over the back of his chair "Morning Bobbin, do you want some porridge before we go?"

"No thank you Grandad, my mummy would not let me out of the house before I ate my breakfast. I'm full up," she said and rubbed her belly.

"Well anyway Gigi's making us a big flask of sweet tea and some cake to take with us," he said finishing his breakfast and putting his plate in the sink. "Let's go and find Alfred, he'll show us the way." Grandad tied the scarf round his neck, put on his storm coat and collected his walking stick from behind the kitchen door.

Gigi kissed them both at the open kitchen door and handed Grandad a canvas bag with their tea and cake inside. Grandad slung the bag over his shoulder, took hold of Bobbin's hand and walked down the garden to the gate and into the Wild Wood.

"Oh, there you are Grandad," said Alfred and dropped down to a lower branch on his ancient oak home. "And Miss Bobbin, did you sleep well last night?" he said with a knowing smile.

Bobbin smiled back. "I did Alfred. My daddy was puzzled though," as the three of them smiled at each other.

Alfred called "Moonbeam, where have you gone?" and turned to Grandad and Bobbin. "He was here a minute ago."

Moonbeam the Otter appeared from behind a fallen tree and sat down just like Bobbin's dog Manu and raised his front legs and smiled at Bobbin.

Alfred puffed out his feathers and said to Grandad "Moonbeam's going to take you to where Reynard is. Blade is there, and the Lord Devon and Oberon are there also, thank heavens," and looked up at the sky. That's plenty of us woodland folk to deal with those High Moor stoats and weasels and their friends the crows. Lord Devon with put them in their place I'm sure."

"Aren't you showing us to Reynard Alfred?" asked Grandad.

"No Grandad, I need to find antiseptic herbs, very rare this time of winter for Reynard. We can't risk my dear friend getting ill with the sepsis. I need to find those herbs quick," said Alfred flapping his wings in his worry.

"Of course!" said Grandad "If you can't find any, we'll take Reynard back to the cottage and I'll have Gigi make up one of her potions."

"An excellent thought Grandad. Thank you so much. But let's all get going and we are to meet at the Secret Lake hopefully very soon. I'm so worried about my Reynard, the scallywag!" Alfred opened his wings and flew off without making a sound.

"Off you go then Moonbeam," called Grandad. The Otter gave a giggle of delight and ran off towards the High Moor. "Not too fast Moonbeam, Bobbin and I have only two legs, you have four."

Moonbeam looked round and waited patiently for them to catch up.

"Thank you, Moonbeam," said Bobbin. "I love how fast you can swim. Would you teach me in the summer please?"

"Oh, I would love to Miss Bobbin," and ran off again, stopped a short distance from Grandad and Bobbin and waited for them again.

"We'll swim in the Secret Lake Miss Bobbin. It's very safe and not deep. I taught the fawn Oberon to swim there."

"Only if I or Gigi are there as well Bobbin, you're too young to swim on your own yet," said Grandad. "But what a good idea, thank you Moonbeam."

They came to the beginning of the High Moor and began to climb the gentle slope onto the moorland. The day was quite cold, the wind even colder, the sky grey and threatening. Moonbeam seemed not to notice, but Grandad pulled his cap tighter on his head and adjusted his scarf round his ears and Bobbin took a woollen hat from her coat pocket, put it on and pulled the coat's hood over her head.

"I think we'll both have a cup of Gigi's sweet tea when we get to Reynard, that'll keep us warm for the journey back. How are you feeling Bobbin?" said Grandad looking at Bobbin closely.

"I'm really enjoying it Grandad. Perhaps we can share Gigi's cake with our friends when we get there," she replied and took Grandad's hand and walked on behind Moonbeam.

"We're nearly there Bobbin, let's hope that rascal Reynard is not too badly hurt," said Grandad frowning.

Oberon was waiting on the end path as it wound its way through an ancient oak wood with stands of alder and ash trees on the edges of the wood. The ground was strewn with rocks both large and small that were covered in mosses, liverworts and lichen. In the springtime when all the plants came back to life after their long winter sleep, the whole wood would be carpeted in bluebells, giving a magical and expectant feeling to the animals of the High Moor, for they knew that fairies live there.

"Grandad," said Bobbin "Why have we not been here before, it's such a lovely place."

"It is Bobbin. Can you feel the magic?" replied Grandad. "That's why Moonbeam is staying so close to us. He's nervous." Moonbeam stopped and looked round at Grandad who said quietly "Don't be afraid Moonbeam they are our friends."

"Yes he is Grandad isn't he," said Bobbin, "and I feel that we are being watched. I'm not frightened, for something is telling me whatever is hiding in the wood are our friends. But why are they hiding from us?" she said as the sound of many small creatures whispering to each other, came to her ears.

"They are the fairies of the Oak Wood Bobbin, they will show themselves to me but only when I'm alone. You have to give them time to get used to you first but maybe not today though. Let's get on," he said and told Moonbeam to hurry up.

As they came out of the oak wood they saw Oberon waiting and both Grandad and Bobbin waved at the young Red Deer who raised his head in greeting as both Grandad and Bobbin distinctly heard the sound of many voices saying just above a whisper "Come back and see us soon Miss Bobbin."

Bobbin stopped and turned to Grandad wide-eyed in astonishment and happiness "Grandad."

Grandad smiled "Yes Bobbin that is the oak wood fairies, they must have heard me saying your name, isn't that wonderful."

"Oh, Grandad I'll have to come back and see them. Can I?" she said earnestly.

"Yes, we will come back here at Christmas Time, I always come here then. Gigi makes them a big cake," Grandad said to the waiting Oberon a warm and formal greeting.

"Greetings Grandad, so good to see you again." replied Oberon and looked at Bobbin shyly and said "I see you Miss Bobbin, you have grown bigger since we last met." It had been a few weeks earlier when Oberon had been lost on the High Moor worrying his parents and all the Wild Wood folk.

"Hello Oberon, I am very pleased to see you also and yes, I have grown a bit. My daddy says I'm going through a growing spurt," and she laughed. "But Oberon, what are those bumps on your head?" Bobbin asked, frowning.

Oberon raised his eyes as if trying to see the top of his head, then lifted his head proudly and said to Bobbin "They are my antlers that are beginning to grow at last Miss Bobbin. This time next year they will be the size of my father's." Then he shook his head again and said "Well maybe not quite as big as my father's," and smiled at Bobbin.

"They will be in another two or three seasons Oberon. But we must get on and see to Reynard," said Grandad, beginning to worry again about the fox.

Further up the path the three of them came across Blade the Badger sitting patiently on a large stone at the side of the path. He stood as they appeared and stepped down to the path and greeted them all in his own grumpy badger way.

"There you are Grandad, I've been up here all night listening to those stoats and weasels talking about what they are going to do to Reynard, just because he comes from the Wild Wood. Would you believe it?" and stood legs apart and arms folded, showing how angry he was. "I think it's about time we called a gathering of the countryside folk. Yes, I'm going to speak to the Lord Devon on it!" and stamped his feet.

"Yes Blade," said Grandad, "but can you show us where Reynard and Lord Devon are first, please?"

"Oh, yes, silly me. Come this way," Blade replied and turned and ran down the path a short distance, stopped and pointed. There by the small mountain stream they saw the Lord Devon, who raised his head to them in greeting then continued to speak with a crow who sat on one of the branches of an oak tree at the edge of the stream.

As they came nearer to the Lord Devon the Crow flew away and there was Reynard the Fox sitting under the tree holding an injured paw up against his chest, his expression an overdone *Poor me* when he saw Grandad and Bobbin.

Blade said "I think he's putting it on Grandad, he looks twice as bad as he did a few minutes ago," he grumbled.

Grandad smiled at Blade and said "Give me one moment Blade," and stepped up to the Lord Devon and said formally "Greetings my Lord Devon, I am pleased to see you once more. I hope you and Titania are both well and how young Oberon grows," and put his arm over Bobbin's shoulder "You know Bobbin of course my Lord."

"I do indeed," said the Lord Devon and lifted his antlers high in a majestic salute. "I greet you Miss Bobbin, we must meet more often when you get older. How are your parents? Well, I hope?"

Bobbin, as in the first time she met the Lord Devon, was taken aback by his regal appearance and size, swallowed to find her courage which gave her time to think of her answer, then when she was sure she was ready, looked the Red Deer in the eye and said: "Thank you Lord Devon, my parents are both well and I look forward to seeing both you and the Lady Titania again soon."

"Then in the summertime when the days are warmer and longer Miss Bobbin, we will look forward to that." The Lord Devon smiled at Bobbin then turned to Grandad once more.

"Perhaps you had better look at Reynard," Lord Devon said to Grandad, "I don't think it's anything really serious though."

Grandad stepped over to Reynard who held out his injured paw for Grandad and looked at him with tearful eyes. "Is it really serious Grandad? Will I ever be able to run again?"

"Well let me have a look at it. Come over here Bobbin and see this," said Grandad kneeling down beside Reynard and took his paw in his hand and looked closely at it.

Reynard looked up at Bobbin and said tearfully "My paw hurts Miss Bobbin."

Bobbin smiled at Reynard and stroked her hand over his head and said "Don't worry Reynard, Grandad will know what to do."

Grandad stood and looked over at the Lord Devon and Blade. "It's not broken, but he needs to rest it for a few days," and smiled at them both. "He's putting it on a bit though. I'll take him back to the cottage. He'll be better in no time with some of Gigi's stew and a hot poultice or two and Alfred's herbs."

"Umph!" grumbled Blade, "I thought so Grandad, he's a scallywag I know, but I will miss him terribly if anything happens to him."

"So would I Lord Devon," agreed Moonbeam the Otter, who had been looking at his old friend with a worried expression on his handsome face.

The Lord Devon stepped forward and said "How peculiar, everyone calls him a scallywag and yet at the same time everyone likes him," and said to Reynard "I am pleased you are not too badly hurt, you scallywag Reynard."

Everyone laughed including Reynard the Fox who said "Thank you my Lord," and forced another tear to dribble down his cheek.

"Where does he live?" asked Bobbin, "So I can keep an eye on him when he gets better."

Blade replied "He has a chamber in my set Miss Bobbin. He's very untidy though. I have to continually clean up after him and I get no thanks at all Miss Bobbin."

Grandad, who had been thinking and making up his mind, said to the Lord Devon "Would you my Lord Devon allow young Oberon to carry Reynard on his back to my cottage?"

"An excellent idea Grandad," said Lord Devon and turned to his son Oberon who had already thought of the idea and nodded to his father and then Grandad.

"But first my Lord, let Bobbin and I drink our hot sweet tea and we have some of Gigi's cake for you all," said Grandad.

Later Grandad picked up the fox and placed him gently on Oberon's back. "Is that not too heavy for you?" he said to the young Red deer.

"I can hardly feel him Grandad," Oberon replied, looking at his father with pride.

"Then let us proceed to Grandad's cottage everyone," commanded the Lord Devon, "It is some distance from here.

"What about the stoats and weasels and those bullies the Crows," said the worried Blade.

"I have spoken to Talon the Crow who is the tribal chief of the High Moorland Crows and he agrees that this nonsense must stop and will arrange for a gathering," spoke the Lord Devon with all his authority and majesty.

....

It was late afternoon when they reached the back garden gate of Grandad's cottage. Gigi had been told they were on their way by Hernshaw the Heron who had been told by Flash the Kingfisher who had been told by one of the High Moorland crows and had flown to the Secret Lake to tell his friend Hernshaw.

"There you all are," cried Gigi as they all appeared from the Wild Wood. "Good afternoon, Lord Devon, I am delighted to see you once more, and look at young Oberon, "Hasn't he grown and so strong now." She looked at the fox who had put on the *Poor me* expression on his face once more as soon as he saw Gigi as she gave the fox a hug.

Grandad lifted Reynard off Oberon's back. "I'll put him in my shed" and said to Reynard "You'll be nice and warm in there Reynard and Gigi will bring you her Countryside Stew, I think you'll like that my friend."

"We had better leave Grandad I can hear a car coming," spoke the Lord Devon. "I thank you once more on behave of all the animals of the Wild Wood for your and Miss Bobbin's assistance." He looked at Bobbin and

49

said "Let us see each other again at our Christmas gathering in the Oak Wood. I'll speak with the fairies they know your name." Lord Devon smiled and with all the other animals went back into the Wild Wood.

Grandad called to Blade, "Come and see me the next full moon Blade, Reynard should be ready to go home about then."

"I will Grandad, I will," called Blade.

And on breeze Grandad, Gigi and Bobbin heard Oberon call from the Wild Wood, "Goodbye Miss Bobbin, I'll see you at Yuletide or sooner."

They all smiled at each other as a car stopped outside the cottage "That will be my Daddy," said Bobbin.

The Gathering

Alfred the Owl had circled Bobbin's house three times before her bedroom light came on, telling the owl that Bobbin was now in her room. He silently landed on her window sill and looked through the window into her bedroom.

Bobbin by then was lying on her bed, comfortably propped up on pillows reading a book. She was dressed in pyjamas that were patterned from top to bottom in embroidered images that looked to Alfred as if they were all the woodland folk that lived in the Wild Wood and, there in the centre of her pyjama top, over her heart was a large embroidery of himself.

How wonderful, she loves us all he thought and gently tapped on the window with his beak hoping Bobbin's Mummy and Daddy would not hear the noise he had made.

He knew at night, in the dark, sound, any sound made by any living creature, would travel much further and be heard by so many others than it did during the daylight hours. Even the smallest of sounds made by the smallest of folk in the Wild Wood could be heard by all the woodland folk from one end of the wood, across the Secret Lake to the other side of the Wild Wood in the darkness.

Bobbin looked up from her book as soon as she heard Alfred's first tap on the window pane and slapped her book down on the quilt, leapt from her bed and ran to the window.

Alfred was delighted seeing the happy and excited look on Bobbin's pretty face, telling him she was very pleased to see him, and flapped his wings and puffed out his feathers in greeting as Bobbin opened the window.

"Now Miss Bobbin," said Alfred seriously, "put your dressing gown on, it's so very cold out here. Grandad is always complaining he has caught another cold in this season of the year," and gave her his best smile, a smile he only gave to those he loved.

Bobbin ran to her bedroom door and Alfred saw an even larger picture on the back of her pyjama top of the Lord Devon, his Lady Titania and their son Oberon as she took her dressing gown from its hook and ran back to Alfred.

"That's better Miss Bobbin," said Alfred. "Oh and good evening. Are you well? he asked politely.

Bobbin smiled "Yes thank you Alfred."

"And your Mummy and Daddy Miss Bobbin?" Alfred asked, gently pressing her for news of her parents.

"They are both well thank you," answered Bobbin patiently. She had learnt over the past year since getting to know the woodland folk, especially Alfred, that the formalities must be observed first, even before the most important of messages are delivered.

"Well Miss Bobbin," said Alfred "it's been some days now since we have last spoken, and I know Grandad will be speaking to your Mummy and Daddy later this evening." He flapped his wings once and paused briefly thinking on the words he had to say: "It's the Yuletide Gathering in the Oak Wood where the fairies live," and paused again. "The Fairy Queen has told me it will be held on your Christmas Eve this year," and looked at Bobbin questionably "As you know Miss Bobbin, us woodland folk call this time of year Yuletide," and flapped his wings once again to show how important it all was to everyone.

Bobbin thought for a moment before answering Alfred's concerns. "I know we are, that's my Mummy and Daddy and myself" (and pointed to herself) "are spending Christmas Day and Boxing Day at Grandad's and Gigi's cottage." She paused again thinking on it more. Then satisfied, she continued "I'll ask Grandad and Gigi to ask my Mummy and Daddy if I could come to them two days earlier, so I can help them prepare for the Gathering and help Gigi to bake her Wild Wood Christmas Cake."

The delighted Alfred was so pleased he could hardly contain his excitement. "Miss Bobbin! I had hoped you would say that. The Fairy Queen told me she is really looking forward to meeting you again." Alfred flapped his wings and puffed out his feathers and said seriously: "Those High Moor crows and their friends the stoats and weasels are saying they are going to be naughty and try to spoil the Yuletide Gathering." He looked at Bobbin closely and said quietly, "But the Lord Devon and his son Oberon have other ideas."

"And Grandad as well Alfred, I expect he will be speaking to Lord Devon," added Bobbin seriously.

"Well yes, Miss Bobbin. I know he's spoken to Lord Devon already this week and plans to meet again the day before Yuletide, that's your Christmas Eve, and they want Bardon the Badger and his brother Blade, myself and that scallywag Reynard and now hopefully you. Oberon told me he's looking forward to seeing you again." Alfred smiled at Bobbin and looked up at the moon, "I must get on; time moves on so quickly these cold winter days don't you think so Miss Bobbin? Oh, by the way, Miss Bobbin, who made your pyjamas?"

"Gigi" replied Bobbin.

"Gigi! Of course, of course she did," and opened his wings and flew off in the same silence as when he arrived.

"Goodnight Alfred," called Bobbin and closed her window, returned her dressing gown to the hook on her bedroom door and got into bed. The bedroom was now quite chilly.

In the morning at breakfast, Bobbin sat at the kitchen table with her Daddy, both of them watching Mummy cook their breakfast. This morning they were having boiled eggs and toast. She really enjoyed Mummy's soft-boiled eggs, she did them just as Bobbin liked and would always pull Daddy's leg saying "Your eggs Daddy are either too hard or too soft and runny. Best let Mummy cook them."

Her Daddy laughed saying, "I think you're right there, Bobbin. Best let Mummy cook them." Then he asked "What's that book you were reading last night? And I thought I heard you speaking to someone."

"It's Grandad's book he wrote on the lives of the woodland animals," she replied. "I was reading it out loud. Did I disturb you?" and crossed her fingers and asked forgiveness for the little white lie she had just told.

"Not at all my lovely girl," said Daddy, who leaned over the table and kissed the top of her head. "And yes, I remember Grandad wrote that when I wasn't much older than you are now," and smiled at the memory. "Are you enjoying it?"

"Yes, I am Daddy," and smiled at her secret knowledge.

"Here you are," said Mummy putting a plate down in front of Bobbin and Daddy "Fresh boiled eggs straight from Gigi's free-range woodland chickens."

"Oh, by the way," said Daddy, "Grandad called me last night, you were asleep, and asked if you could be at the cottage three days before Christmas to help Gigi make her Wild Wood Cake. Would you like that?" and picked up his butter knife and sliced off the top of one of his eggs. "Mummy and daddy will be at Grandad and Gigi's on Christmas Day morning."

Bobbin pretended to think for a moment, and after saying "Err" then unable to hide her excitement any longer "Oh yes please Daddy!" hiding her smile behind her hand. "You won't forget to bring my Christmas presents, will you?"

"Have we ever forgotten your Christmas presents Bobbin?" Daddy said laughing at the thought. "That's settled then. It'll give Mummy and me a chance to do some Christmas shopping," he said happily.

....

"The Fairy Queen has spoken to Bardon the Badger," said Grandad, as Gigi helped Bobbin off with her coat. "She tells Bardon she's really pleased you will be at the Gathering."

Grandad paused and looked at her closely. "Queen Celandine says you are special Bobbin."

Bobbin frowned in puzzlement and wrinkled up her nose, "Special Grandad, what does that mean?"

Grandad thought for a moment wondering how he was to explain it to her and placed his hands on her shoulders as Gigi took her hand in hers and said quietly "Bobbin, you have the Gift," and knew she would have to explain further. "You already know things about the animals in the Wild Wood and are able to speak with them."

Bobbin smiled and nodded her understanding. "They know you have the Gift. The fairies know you have the Gift. Both Grandad and I have the Gift. That's how we" (and looked at Grandad) "and all the animals of the Wild Wood recognised it in you," and kissed the top of her head.

Bobbin smiled knowingly at Grandad and Gigi, "My Mummy and Daddy do not have the Gift, do they?"

"No Bobbin they don't," answered Grandad. "My Mummy and Daddy didn't have it either. But Gigi's Mummy and Daddy did and my grandparents to!" He looked up at the clock on the wall, "We're meeting the Lord Devon at the Secret Lake in an hour. Let's have some sweet tea before we leave."

....

Grandad opened the garden gate at the back of the cottage and they stepped onto the path that led into the Wild Wood and suddenly it seemed that out of nowhere appeared all the small woodland animals. Bobbin looked up at Grandad who smiled to her and said "I thought they might be waiting for us. Everyone's worried about the Yuletide Gathering."

The Wild Wood folk all began speaking at once with their high-pitched little voices and Bobbin found it hard to understand what they were saying. But Grandad, who was more used to their excited chatter, was and said to Bobbin, "They are saying: Grandad, Bobbin have you heard the High Moor crows and the stoats, and the weasels are going to be very naughty and spoil the Yuletide Gathering."

The rabbits were hopping on and off the path, some getting themselves almost under the feet of Bobbin who laughed "Now be careful you bunnies." The two tribes of squirrels that lived in the tree tops had come down and were running up and down the tree trunks. The bigger Grey Squirrels and the much smaller Red Squirrels usually would not speak to each other. But the awful news of their Yuletide Gathering had swept their differences aside and they stood together voicing their anger at the High Moor bullies.

Wood mice, Field mice, Door mice and Shrews made their homes among the roots of ancient trees close to the Secret Bank, where Alfred the Owl knew of special herbs and rare wildflowers that loved to grow in its rich, leafy fertile earth. They had all come to see Grandad and Bobbin, happy now knowing their Yuletide Gathering would hopefully be saved and were jumping from one fallen tree branch to the other trying to keep up as Grandad and Bobbin walked into the Wild Wood.

The Wild Wood stoats and weasels, who were so much nicer folk than their High Moor cousins and would never even think of speaking to them, were, as usual, dancing together happily on each side of the path all looking up and shouting "Hello Miss Bobbin. It's lovely to see you again!"

In the lower branches of the trees, it seemed that all the small birds that lived in the Wild Wood were there.

There was a whole tribe of finches, the Green Finches, the Chaffinches, the Gold Finches and the more robust Bullfinches, lining the lower branches along the path. Among them were the smaller Tits, Blue Tits, Coal

Tits, Great Tits, Long Tailed Tits and even the Crested Tits felt it was important enough to make an appearance. While the even smaller and most difficult to see were the Tree Creepers and Nuthatches who lived on the trunks of the bigger trees, all loudly calling their greeting to Bobbin and, sat on the path as it winded its way deeper into the Wild Wood, waited Reynard the Fox.

Bobbin smiled and waved at them all which made them all shout and sing even louder so that Grandad and Bobbin were unable to listen any more and put their fingers in their ears.

Then suddenly Reynard gave a loud "Yelp!" and all the Wild Wood animals and small birds fell silent and looked at Reynard.

"That's better," said Reynard, pleased with himself, and trotted along the path to Grandad and Bobbin, stopped in front of them, puffed up his chest to show how important he was and gazed politely at Grandad.

Grandad turned to Bobbin and said in a whisper "We must always observe the formalities, Bobbin."

Bobbin nodded her understanding for she knew she must take these preambles seriously.

"Good morning, Reynard, how nice seeing you again so soon" for it had only been a short time since Grandad had taken the injured fox back to his lodgings at Blade the Badger's set. Then taking Bobbin's hand in his said "You remember my Great Grand Daughter Bobbin?"

"Good morning, Grandad, Miss Bobbin. I am pleased to see you both," and gave one of his rare sincere smiles to Bobbin.

"How's your leg?" asked Bobbin.

"Thank you for asking Miss Bobbin. It is all mended now, thanks to Gigi and Grandad," replied Reynard courteously. "How are your parents?

The woodland animals were becoming impatient and began talking amongst themselves, their voices becoming louder and louder again. The stoats and weasels were even heard calling to Reynard "Get on with it you scallywag!"

Reynard gave another sharp loud "Yelp!" and the animals and birds fell silent again.

"I do apologise for my woodland cousins' rudeness Grandad," said Reynard. "But all my friends are worried that our Yuletide Gathering is going to be spoilt by the stoats and weasels from the High Moor, and especially those crows."

"Bobbin and I are off to meet with the Lord Devon at the Secret Lake," replied Grandad, "to make our plans to stop this nonsense."

Reynard felt so very pleased with himself for having this so very important conversation with Grandad. "Yes I know Grandad" and pointed with his chin to all the woodland animals now silent and listening to what the fox was saying. "We are here to escort you to the Secret Lake. Aren't we?" and looked at all the waiting impatient animals and birds.

"Yes, we are Grandad, Miss Bobbin," squeaked and chattered the animals and chirped the birds excitedly.

Reynard gave one of his not so loud yelps this time and looked at Grandad apologetically and continued "Would you follow me please Grandad, Miss Bobbin." The fox turned and led the way deeper along the path into the Wild Wood.

Bobbin and Grandad both smiled at each other and followed the fox.

Reynard turned his head and said to Bobbin "I can't walk very fast Miss Bobbin my leg still hurts a bit."

Bobbin called to the fox over the chatter of the animals and confused singing of the birds, "I am sorry to hear that Reynard, but I expect it will be better soon," and looked up at Grandad with laughter in her eyes.

Grandad rolled his eyes at Reynard "Come on you scallywag, let's get on," as they both became aware the woodland folk were all together hopping, jumping, running and dancing around them. Bobbin looked up into the trees and saw the small birds flying from branch to bough, all singing their different songs.

....

They came to a small clearing with high rock walls almost surrounding them. The walls were covered with ivy, small bushes, long grasses and winter plants, with narrow ledges where the woodland birds would find a warm place to rest throughout the cold winter nights and in several places small caves where animals of the Wild Wood such as the stoats and weasels would line with grasses and bracken and wait until the springtime out of the freezing winds, the cold rain and snow. For this was the ancient quarry where Burnet the Little Owl lived, high up, almost at the top of the quarry wall, his warm, cosy home hidden deep among the ivy.

Reynard gave a polite "Yelp" to Burnet, who was hidden without hiding among the ivy leaves and tufted grasses, his feathers of different subtle shades of browns, greys and ivories blending perfectly with the morning's freckled winter sunlight.

Burnet dropped down from the high cliff and called to them from the lowest branch of a small Crab Apple tree now bare of its summer leaves and fruit, some of its branches still edged with the night's frost. "I heard you all coming as soon as you left Grandad's cottage garden Reynard," said Burnet reproachfully. "What a noise you all make. Good morning, Grandad, Miss Bobbin, how nice to see you both again. Are you both well?"

"Yes, we are, thank you Burnet," answered Grandad and Bobbin smiled at the Little Owl and said "Hello". Before Grandad could say any more Reynard the Fox impatiently said to Burnet "You must tell Alfred we will be with him shortly!"

Bobbin stifled a laugh and Grandad smiled his patient smile as Burnet replied seriously "I only take messages from Alfred or Grandad or the Lord Devon himself," and looked at Grandad ignoring Reynard.

Reynard dropped his head in embarrassment realising he had made a mistake and had gone too far. All the animals and birds nearby had heard his blunder and were now laughing at his discomfort.

Grandad seeing Reynard's shame took pity and said "Thank you my good friend Reynard you have been a great help to us. Will you please come with us to the Secret Lake to see the Lord Devon?"

Reynard's head came up immediately and smiled at Grandad's kindness as all the woodland animals and birds fell silent.

Bobbin said quietly to the fox, although just loud enough for all the other animals and birds to hear,

"Reynard would you walk with me? I would be so very pleased."

Reynard blinked at Bobbin's flattery and walked over to Bobbin and sat next to her.

Grandad looked up at Burnet and asked politely "Would you fly to the Secret Lake, your cousin Alfred is waiting for us and the Lord Devon to arrive. Tell him we will be there shortly and Reynard will guide us."

"Yes, Grandad I will," and with a smile to Bobbin, Burnet launched himself out of the Crab Apple tree and flew off into the Wild Wood.

....

They stepped out of the woodland into an open meadow where in the centre was the ancient Oak Tree where Alfred lived. Bobbin looked up at the top branches to where there was a large bowl-shaped opening where Alfred would spend most of the cold and freezing days of winter.

"It must be very cold for Alfred these chilly nights Grandad, couldn't you let him into your shed?" said Bobbin, worried about Alfred's comfort. "He must be older than you Grandad."

Grandad laughed, but at the same time pleased with Bobbin's concern for his oldest woodland friend. "Bobbin," he said, "Alfred knows he has a home in my shed any time he feels like he needs to." They walked on along the path and entered the Wild Wood once more at the other side of the meadow followed and surrounded by all the animals and birds.

....

In half the time it took them all to reach Alfred's oak they came to an even older oak tree and there hidden among dense bramble and bracken was where Blade the Badger, Bardon's brother lived, deep inside a small, ancient mound of earth he shared with Reynard, cosy and warm inside his chamber. Grandad looked down at the fox and asked "Reynard please go and knock-on Blade's door and say we're outside."

The fox yelped his delight on being asked to help and disappeared down the entrance tunnel towards Blade's chamber.

Grandad and Bobbin heard Blade's grumbling before he arrived at the entrance to his set "Yes, yes Grandad, I've been waiting for you..." then Blade spotted Bobbin standing behind Grandad and remembered his manners "Oh Miss Bobbin, I didn't see you there. How are you, well I hope?"

Bobbin replied, "Hello Blade, lovely to see you again and yes I am well thank you."

Reynard appeared from the tunnel and said impatiently "We had better get on, don't want to keep the Lord Devon waiting," and ignoring the grumpy badger stuck his nose in the air and lead the way towards the Secret Lake leaving Grandad and Blade shaking their heads and Bobbin giggling quietly to herself.

....

Talon the Crow was old and tired. He had grown bigger and stronger than all the other crows on the High Moor and was now their High Chief. His feathers were long and black, as black as the darkest of nights, and when in flight they displayed oily iridescent colours that would change shape and glow in the sunlight. He had lived longer, much longer than others of his tribe and had gained wisdom with age and wanted none of this bad behaviour by others of his tribe.

Nor had he ever really liked those stoats and weasels who would constantly be making mischief, not only among themselves that would interrupt the natural peaceful rhythm of the High Moor but also between other moorland animals, such as the small Roe Deer and the gentle Fallow Deer. They were bullied while feeding and being frightened by the younger naughtier crows who would bate them from the air. Talon knew he needed help to stop all this nonsense.

Talon's home was a branch of a high and massive cedar tree that stood at the very edge of the river where in the springtime he would watch the salmon run to lay their eggs much further up river. Although not deep, the river had many dark pools where moorland otters would fish in the fast-flowing water. These otters were Moonbeam's cousins and would have nothing to do with any of Talon's people.

The cedar gave Talon a comfortable place to sit and rest and to ponder over this problem, especially now in the winter time as the High Moor suffered from a bitterly chill wind that blew off the hills that were even higher than the High Moor. Here he was kept warm, almost entirely surrounded by thick, dense clusters of cedar leaves keeping the wind and cold from him.

He knew he needed an ally, a friend from the Wild Wood that would help him find a solution and so he sat and thought while watching a moorland heron fishing at the river's edge and an idea slowly came to him.

Talon dropped down to a lower branch and waited a while, then finally making up his mind said:

"Hello Patience, can I come down and speak with you?" asked Talon.

Patience the Heron turned his head and looked up at the crow asking himself *Should I have anything to do with this old rogue?* thought for another moment and decided he would at least listen to the crow and said "You can come down here Talon but behave yourself."

"I will, thank you Patience," and the crow flew down and landed at the river's edge in a flutter of feathers to find he was looking up at Patience who loomed above him, his long, strong, powerful beak pointing at him disapprovingly.

Patience was tall for a heron, much taller and bigger than his woodland cousin Hernshaw. He too was old now, the same age as Talon the Crow who he had disliked and mistrusted for as long as he had made his home on the High Moor. His friend Hernshaw had made his home in the Wild Wood and fished most of the time at the Secret Lake. They rarely visited each other these cold winter days preferring to stay close to their comfortable heronries until that wonderful and magical time of spring returned and the days grew longer and warmer.

Although they would constantly keep in touch with each other by asking their close friend the swift-winged Flash the Kingfisher to deliver their messages. Patience the High Moor Heron was aware how angry and concerned all the woodland folk were with the threats of High Moor naughtiness and the spoiling of their Yuletide Gathering.

Talon the Crow bowed his head showing his respect to Patience and spoke quietly, "Thank you for agreeing to speak to me my old friend."

The big heron raised both wings ordering the crow to silence. "We are not old friends Talon. We have never been friends. So let us not begin this conversation on a misunderstanding," and folded his wings once more to the side of his body signalling that Talon could continue.

Moonbeam who had been visiting his High Moor cousins was hiding in the reeds close to where his friend Patience had been fishing and giggled to himself.

"My apologies Patience, I am here to ask for your help," said Talon. "I am old now and feel the power I once had among my tribe is fading, others are waiting to take on my mantle. But I want to stop this nonsense of the spoiling of Wild Wood Yuletide Gathering and ask, would you send a message to your cousin Hernshaw and ask him to tell Alfred I will do anything to help," and lowered his head again waiting for Patience's answer.

There was a pause while the heron thought over the crow's request. Talon raised his head slowly and looked into the heron's eyes saying nothing.

At last Patience spoke: "I know you are there, Moonbeam. Come over here," and turned his head and looked in the direction of Moonbeam's hiding place.

Moonbeam lifted his head above the reeds and looked at his friend the heron. "I was hiding Patience. How did you know I was here?" and tutted to himself.

"Of course, I knew you were hiding in the reeds you silly otter," said Patience.

Moonbeam splashed out of the reeds and sat on the bank. "But how did you know I was hiding. No one else knows when I'm hiding!" he said, angrier with himself than the heron.

"The fairies told me then," said Patience impatiently rolling his eyes to the sky.

"Well," said Moonbeam feeling relieved, "why didn't you say so? The fairies! Of course."

"Fairies my beak!" said Talon, "I saw you hiding in the reeds myself. Call yourself an otter," and sneered at Moonbeam.

"Silence Talon!" shouted Patience angrily, "I warned you to behave yourself."

The crow dropped his head once more and stared at the ground hoping the heron would still help him.

"Yes, silence Talon," said Moonbeam sarcastically, mimicking his friend Patience.

"Oh, do shut up Moonbeam," snapped the heron. "Now I want you to run to the Secret Lake and tell Alfred that Talon the Crow asks to speak to him urgently about the Yuletide Gathering," and looked at Talon and then at Moonbeam. "And tell Alfred to send Flash the Kingfisher with his answer. Flash is faster than you are Moonbeam."

"Thank you, Patience," said the crow.

"Don't thank me yet. You haven't had Alfred's answer," advised the heron and turned to Moonbeam. "What are you still doing here? Get yourself off to the Secret Lake you silly otter."

"Talon," said Patience seriously, "I will return to your Cedar Tree here when I have Alfred's answer, do not keep me waiting," and flew off upriver to his favourite beach where he knew the river crayfish hid among the rocks.

....

Hernshaw the Heron stood at the edge of the Secret Lake as Grandad, Bobbin and Reynard the Fox stepped out of the wood and Hernshaw flapped his wings in greeting.

"Hello Grandad and Miss Bobbin, lovely to see you both again," and looked at the fox and said, "Reynard, why is your nose stuck up in the air?"

Grandad quickly answered for the fox: "My friend Reynard has been very helpful and guided us here. I don't know what we would have done without him. Do we Bobbin?"

Bobbin replied eagerly, "No Grandad, we don't."

Moonbeam having just arrived from the High Moor lifted his head out of the water next to Hernshaw and said "Well I do," and laughed out loud, clapped his paws together and swam out into the lake.

All the woodland animals that had followed Grandad and Bobbin to the Secret Lake began to laugh as Hernshaw flapped his great wings ordering them to silence.

"Enough!" Hernshaw cried. "Reynard, Grandad and Miss Bobbin say you have been very helpful and I will tell that to Alfred who will tell the Lord Devon himself."

Reynard the Fox was speechless with pride and stuck his nose even higher in the air.

Hernshaw said "Grandad, Miss Bobbin, Alfred and Bardon the badger are waiting across the lake for you both. Reynard, please show them to the Sacred Grove. The Lord Devon will be there shortly, please hurry."

So off they went once more walking round the lake to the meeting at the Sacred Grove, while Moonbeam the Otter swam and Hernshaw the Heron flew across the lake, all meeting together again just as the Lord Devon with the

Lady Titania and Oberon stepped out of the woodland and held their heads high in greeting to their woodland friends.

They all came together at the Sacred Grove which was hidden among the oaks back from the small beach at the top of the lake. The grove had been a place where even before Roman times Druids of the old religion would gather and pray to their ancient gods and woodland spirits which controlled and enabled all the natural forces that gave and sustained life. It was so that all the animals and birds of the countryside, especially the fairies, knew these old gods of the country folk were still among them, sometimes playing their mischief and tricks on the country folk.

In the Grove, the Lord Devon stood behind an ancient rock altar that stood in the centre of the grove where his father's father, then his father had stood and addressed important Gatherings. Titania and Oberon were standing on his right side behind him.

Bobbin saw and greeted Lord Devon formally by standing straight, her arms at her side and lowering her head. The greeting came naturally and unconsciously to her and she saw Lord Devon's approving smile and the shake of his antlers. To the Lady Titania and Oberon, she greeted them with a warm smile of friendship. They both eagerly smiled back, Titania nodded her head while Oberon proudly shook his growing antlers.

All the Wild Wood animals and birds that had escorted them to the Secret Lake were lining the edges of the Grove, silent and wide-eyed waiting patiently for their Lord Devon to speak.

Grandad took Bobbin's hand and squeezed it gently in approval of her greeting to Lord Devon and looked down at her and smiled, "Well done my lovely girl." Bobbin looked and saw Alfred the Owl with his cousin Burnet the Little Owl both sitting on a low branch of one of the oaks to the left of Lord Devon. They both flapped their wings at her and Grandad, while Bardon and his brother Blade raised a paw at them both. With them sitting under Alfred and Burnet's branch was Reynard the Fox, whose nose was no longer up in the air, as Bardon had told him not to be such a silly fox.

Hernshaw the Heron and Moonbeam the Otter were stood in front of the ancient rock waiting for the Lord Devon to give them permission to speak.

Lord Devon spoke quietly to Grandad, "Greetings Grandad, Miss Bobbin," and looked round at the Lady Titania and Oberon, "we welcome you both to this Gathering."

"Thank you, Lord Devon" and before Grandad could continue both Lady Titania and Oberon quickly stepped forward, "Hello Miss Bobbin, lovely to see you again."

"And you," called Bobbin before Lord Devon sharply turned his head in their direction showing his disapproval for breaking the formalities.

The three friends fell silent and Titania and Oberon stepped back to their places. Grandad put a gentle hand on Bobbin's shoulder and quietly said "Shoosh," and the Lord Devon smiled his smile of indulgence at Grandad, who returned his smile.

Then Lord Devon lifted his head and said to all those gathered at the Sacred Grove "I call on my dear friend Hernshaw the Heron to speak, you have news for us all."

The heron gathered himself and addressed his Lord loud enough for all the woodland folk gathered in the Grove to hear. "Lord Devon" and bowed his head in respect "my friend Moonbeam here" and looked down at the Otter briefly who giggled and wagged his tail, then looked up again at the huge Red Deer "has given me a message from Talon the chieftain of the High Moor Crows to give to you," and bowed his head again waiting for Lord Devon's reply.

"I thank you both," said Lord Devon. "Alfred and I have spoken on this and we are inclined to listen to Talon this once," and looked over at Grandad and asked: "Grandad, not for the first time I ask your opinion on this matter."

Grandad stepped forward leaving Bobbin a step behind him and said "That is an excellent idea, Lord Devon. Talon the Crow shows his respect for you by sending this message." Grandad thought for a few moments and said, "Perhaps you would consider commanding Talon he must bring with him both Larkspur, the leader of the Weasels and Mouse Ear, the leader of the Stoats with him when we speak so you may show them both your anger," said Grandad and stepped back next to Bobbin.

Lord Devon raised his head high and shook his antlers at Grandad in a sign of his agreement and said "Thank you Grandad. Once again you show us your wisdom and love." He turned to his trusted adviser sat quietly on the oak branch and asked, "Alfred my friend, are you in agreement with this plan?"

"Indeed, my Lord. I should have thought of this myself," and flapped his wings eagerly.

"And so dear Alfred please send Flash the Kingfisher back to Patience the High Moor Heron with our answer adding all three of them, the Crow, the Weasel and the Stoat must be here by noon today!" instructed the Red Deer.

....

Flash the Kingfisher found Patience fishing for crayfish at his favourite part of the river and passed on Lord Devon's message just as Alfred had told him. Patience asked the Kingfisher to wait while he spoke to Talon.

Talon the Crow dropped down from his branch high in the cedar tree as soon as he saw Patience land under the tree and dropped his head in a sign of respect and waited for the heron to speak.

As usual there were no pleasantries between them and Patience came straight to the point.

"Talon, I am instructed by the Lord Devon to tell you he will hear you speak. But there is a condition that Larkspur and Mouse Ear are there also and all three of you are to be at the Sacred Grove by noon. I will have your reply now Talon," and looked at the crow who had his head down looking at the ground.

Talon looked up sharply and spoke quickly. "I shall be there at that time Patience and I will order the Weasel and the Stoat to come with me. Please tell the Lord Devon."

"Then use your time to find Larkspur and Mouse Ear," and opened his wings and flew off to pass Talon's message on to Kingfisher.

....

The Lord Devon looked over at Grandad and Bobbin "Let us rest under the tree where Alfred and the badger brothers are seated," and looked down at Hernshaw and Moonbeam "Would you both join us?" then left the rock and walked over to where Alfred was.

The Lady Titania with Oberon and Bobbin eagerly came together in a rush. Bobbin put her arms round them both as the Red Deer laid their heads against Bobbin's shoulders.

"My dear Lady Titania, I am so pleased to see you again," said Bobbin tearfully.

"My dearest Bobbin, it's so lovely to see you once more, and we will see each other again at the Fairy Gathering at Yuletide," gasped Titania in a broken voice.

"Yes," said Oberon and stood back, his head held high, "and do you like my antlers Miss Bobbin?"

"They grow Oberon, they grow. You look wonderful," said Bobbin and put her arms round his neck again affectionally.

"What special Yuletide dress will you be wearing Bobbin?" asked Lady Titania. "Gigi always wears her special dress."

"Gigi hasn't mentioned a special dress for me my Lady," said Bobbin.

The Lady Titania looked shocked and quickly said "Oh dear Bobbin, Gigi must be keeping it a secret until Yuletide, then surprise you. Oh, dear oh dear!"

"Mother!" said Oberon.

Bobbin laughed and said happily "Please don't you worry about that. I won't say a word that I know. We'll have such a happy time at the Gathering."

"Oh, thank you Bobbin, don't tell Gigi though" and smiled a loving smile. "Let us join the others," and walked over to Alfred's tree, the three of them side by side.

Reynard the Fox was waiting and wondering if he should stay. He had not been asked to sit with the others and felt uncomfortable and unsure of what he should do, wondering should he give them room to discuss the coming meeting with the High Moor folk. He began to walk away unhappily when Alfred spoke "Where are you going you scallywag?"

The Lord Devon look round and said "Please join us Reynard, I might need you shortly."

Reynard was so pleased to have been spoken to by the Lord Devon he puffed out his chest in pride and returned to the tree and sat unable to speak, his nose up in the air once more.

The badger brothers Bardon and Blade both shook their heads and smiled at each other.

"Let us rest," declared Lord Devon. Titania, Oberon and Bobbin sat together and talked amongst themselves, while the two badgers, Moonbeam, Reynard and Hernshaw gathered round the Lord Devon and Grandad with Alfred, Burnet his cousin and Flash the Kingfisher looking down from their branch.

....

Talon the Crow fluttered his wings as he flew across the Secret Lake and into the Sacred Grove landing on the short grass in front of the Altar Rock, quickly lowering his head and waited in respectful silence.

The Lord Devon spoke in a hushed voice to his surrounding woodland folk sat with Grandad and Bobbin. "Dear friends, let us listen to Talon the Crow." Alfred flapped his wings and announced, "I can see Larkspur the Weasel and Mouse Ear the Stoat just arriving at the far side of the Secret Lake Lord Devon."

"Ah, I see them, Alfred," and looked round at the fox. "Reynard..." and paused a moment thinking and said, "No, on second thoughts Bardon, Blade, please go and meet with those two bullies and escort them here."

Reynard the Fox dropped his head to his chest in disappointment having been thrilled when the Lord Devon had spoken his name and tearfully watched the two badgers run awkwardly, for badgers cannot run fast, to the path surrounding the lake, both grumbling their anger and excitement and playfully jostling and snapping at each other as they ran.

A tear dribbled down the fox's cheek.

"Reynard!" spoke the Lord Devon loud enough for all the animals and birds at the Sacred Grove to hear "I want you to stand on my right side please, Grandad and Miss Bobbin, at my left side please. Lady Titania and my son," and looked at Titania and Oberon with love and pride in his eyes "on my right side behind Reynard."

Reynard lifted his head flabbergasted, not sure if he had heard the Lord Devon correctly and hesitated and looked up at Alfred in confusion.

Alfred tutted and smiled at Reynard and said "Get over there you silly fox," and whispered to Burnet the Little Owl "Wait here, you will be needed to take Lord Devon's message to the Fairy Queen Celandine."

Burnet puffed out his feathers in pride at taking such an important message from the Lord Devon himself to the Fairy Queen.

"And Alfred, my trusted friend would you put yourself on our Altar Rock and listen to these High Moor bullies and advise me," asked Lord Devon respectfully.

"I will my Lord," and dropped down from his branch landing in the centre of the Altar Rock.

Reynard the Fox found himself in a position of Great Honour at the right side of the Lord Devon at this very formal occasion and once more his nose rose up into the air feeling so very pleased with himself and heard Oberon playfully whisper to him, "Your nose is in the air Reynard, you silly fox."

Reynard quickly lowered his nose as the Lord Devon looked down at him frowning.

Alfred spoke quietly to the crow: "Talon, let us hope this nonsense will be stopped here today. The Lord Devon is very angry at the threats coming from certain High Moor folk."

The crow lifted his head for the first time since arriving at the Sacred Grove and answered "I hope so Alfred, I really do."

....

Larkspur the Weasel and Mouse Ear the Stoat both looked very worried as they followed Bardon and Blade into the Sacred Grove and stopped behind Talon who now stood straight and looked at the Altar Rock ignoring them.

The two fidgeted and stepped from one foot to the other and looked at the Lord Devon with nervous expressions on their faces.

"Stand still! Both of you," said Alfred angrily. "You are in the presence of your Lord Devon." Both Larkspur and Mouse Ear stopped their fidgeting and stood upright, still and wide-eyed.

Bobbin began to feel sorry for them both and took Grandad's hand and whispered "Grandad, are they going to be Told Off?"

Grandad squeezed her hand and said quietly "I would think so Bobbin, they have been very naughty," and bent over and whispered in her ear, "Sometimes Bobbin some folk just have to be Told Off. And a telling off is better than banishment."

Bobbin looked up at her Great Grandfather in confusion and with trembling lips asked, "Grandad, what does banishment mean?"

Grandad now knelt down beside her and said just above a whisper, "It means that if the Lord Devon thinks it's serious enough, he could send them off the High Moor to find somewhere else to live and they cannot return to their homes."

"Oh, dear Grandad," said Bobbin. "Let's hope Lord Devon gives them a Telling Off then," and a tear ran down her cheek.

Grandad noticed and wiped her cheek and kissed the top of her head.

The Lord Devon stepped forward to the Altar Rock and spoke with a powerful, loud voice: "Larkspur and Mouse Ear, you have threatened to spoil our Yuletide Gathering at the Oak Wood. Our Yuletide Gathering has a great symbolic meaning to all those that live in the Wild

Wood, especially our friends the Fairies. How dare you and your friends the crows think of disturbing my peace on my land and frighten my woodland folk!" and violently shook his mighty antlers to show his anger.

All the animals and birds of the Wild Wood who had gathered at the Sacred Grove shuddered at the Lord Devon's anger and hid among the trees and bushes asking each other fearfully what the Lord Devon is going to do with this pair of bullies.

"What do you have to say of your dreadful behaviour?" and shook his antlers once again.

Larkspur and Mouse Ear looked at each other shaking their heads in fear, both wondering what was going to happen to them. Larkspur spoke first crying in despair "It wasn't me Lord Devon, Mouse Ear made me do it."

"No, I didn't, it was your idea. Just for a laugh you said," shouted Mouse Ear and turned to Talon the Crow. "It wasn't me Talon. Please tell Lord Devon."

Talon the Crow remained silent and looked down at the grass.

"We were only joking," cried Larkspur. "It was just a joke."

"Yes, that's right," said Mouse Ear, "we were only joking, weren't we Talon."

The Lord Devon roared in his anger and violently shook his antlers again surprising Alfred and the other animals close by, for they had never seen the Lord Devon shake his antlers more than twice to show his anger.

"Silence!" and the Lord Devon stepped back from the Altar Rock and said to Alfred "Let's gather under the tree again and discuss these two silly High Moor folk and ask Talon the Crow to join us. Tell those two to remain where they are."

....

The Lord Devon stood in the centre as the others of his inner circle of friends gathered around him. Talon the Crow was stood between Alfred and the badger brothers.

"Reynard, I told you to stand by me," said Lord Devon lightly and the fox ran to the Red Deer's side and stuck his nose in the air.

"Talon," said Lord Devon, "What would you have me do with those two," and looked over and saw them both looking over the Altar Rock trying to see what was going on.

Talon responded to the Red Deer's question firmly "Lord Devon, you have given them both fear. Fear is not something they have experienced before. Yes, they are bullies, but now you have frightened the bullying out of them and I ask you this once to give them both a good Telling Off and not banishment. You won't have to speak to them again my Lord," and dropped his head to the ground showing his respect.

The Lord Devon turned to Alfred, "And your advice, my friend."

"Lord Devon, I find myself agreeing with Talon, they are both silly moorland creatures indeed," answered Alfred looking over at the two naughty animals.

"Thank you Alfred," he said and looked at Grandad. "What do you and Miss Bobbin think on this matter?"

Grandad thought for a moment and said "Lord Devon, I see no evil in them, just stupidity. I also say give them a good Telling Off but threaten them with abandonment," and looked down at Bobbin.

Bobbin took a deep breath and said, "I would be so pleased if you would just give them both a Telling Off Lord Devon. After all it is so near Yuletide and I have read it is a forgiving time of year."

"Well said Miss Bobbin," called Oberon excitedly and the Lord Devon looked at his son frowning.

The Lady Titania smiled her agreement at Bobbin.

"Well said Miss Bobbin," spoke the Lord Devon and turned his head and looked at both his Lady Titania and Oberon, "Especially as my family agrees with you, I dare not make any other decision this time" and paused and looked at Talon. "Do you hear me, Talon? I said this time."

Talon the Crow raised his head from the ground "Thank you Lord Devon, I am relieved and now I can Tell Off my own younger crows, they will know how angry you are. And so put an end to this nonsense once and for all."

"Then let us return to the Altar Rock and I will give them a Telling Off," and walked back over to his place at the Rock with the others following behind.

Larkspur the weasel and Mouse Ear the stoat saw the Lord Devon returning to the Rock and stood back and took each other in their arms and fearfully waited for his verdict.

The Lord Devon eyed them both with hard, serious eyes that frightened Larkspur and Mouse Ear even more and then shook his antlers so fiercely that they jumped backwards almost falling over themselves as he announced his verdict.

"Larkspur and Mouse Ear," his voice raising to a roar that left Larkspur and Mouse Ear shaking. "You have been very naughty, so naughty that I feel you should be banished from my lands of the Wild Wood and the High

Moor." Larkspur and Mouse Ear stopped their shaking and stood still, their mouths open in shock, their eyes wide open in awe of their punishment.

"However, I have been persuaded by my good friends here..." He paused and seeing Grandad and Bobbin who he shook his antlers at them, and then at Alfred the Owl whom he also shook his antlers at and looked down at Talon the Crow "and my good friend Talon, to give you a Telling Off instead." He stepped closer to the Rock and looking down at Larkspur and Mouse Ear, who were both now cringing beneath Lord Devon's antlers, and continued:

"This nonsense and bad behaviour will now stop! Not just for Yuletide but for all the seasons of the Wild Wood and the High Moor. Is that understood you two? If I or my friends here today, and that includes my friend Talon the Crow, hear of any more bad behaviour I will immediately banish you both from all my lands. And you will never return."

The Lord Devon stared at them as they both slowly digested what had been said to them, suddenly realising they had not been banished and their ordeal was over and both still in each other's arms jumped for joy and ran off crying out loud to everyone "We're not banished, we're not banished, we're not banished" as they ran round the Secret Lake running faster and faster, leaving the gathered animals and birds laughing.

The Lord Devon looked down at Talon the Crow and said "Talon my friend, for your courage in helping to stop this nonsense you are invited to our Yuletide Gathering in the Fairies Oak Wood and we all look forward to seeing you there" and looked round at all those gathered in the Sacred Grove "Are we not my friends?"

Grandad and Bobbin, along with Alfred the Owl, Burnet the Little Owl, the badger brothers Bardon and Blade, with Moonbeam the Otter and Hernshaw the Heron and Flash the Kingfisher with Reynard the Fox all shouted "Hurrah!" and Talon the Crow lifted his head and said quietly "Thank you all my friends."

"Then off you go Burnet my little friend and tell Queen Celandine all is well," said the Lord Devon and to the others "Let us all return to our homes and prepare ourselves for the Yuletide Gathering! And Reynard, you can take your nose out of the air now."

Yuletide

"Good morning my precious Bobbin," said Gigi as she turned on Bobbin's bedside lamp, "it's almost Yule and we have a wildwood cake to bake and your Yule dress to finish. Up you get."

Bobbin opened her eyes, smiled at her Great Grandmother and looked out of the bedroom window. "Gigi! It's still dark," she complained stretching herself. "I was having such a nice sleep."

Gigi gave her a knowing look. "You always will, you have a good soul and it's almost 8 o'clock. What would you like for breakfast? I've just made Grandad my wildwood pancakes with honey that the bees allowed us to take last summer."

"Ooh, yes please," cried Bobbin as she jumped out of her bed and put her dressing gown on. "Tell Grandad to wait for me, I'll be right down." She ran to her window and saw the sky was clear, the stars still shining brightly. "Gigi do the stars have names like the trees and plants?"

Gigi looked out of the window and up at the sky "There," she pointed, "is the Waning Moon, come New Year, that's next week, we'll have a Full Moon and that cluster of stars over there that's Orion, he's known as the sky's Hunter and there's Taurus the Bull and there's......"

"And so, Gigi," said Bobbin, looking at her Great Grandmother seriously, a look of concentration on her face "why do all our woodland friends make so much of Yuletide? It means so much to them, but I don't think I really understand why."

Gigi gave her a loving smile and took her face gently in her hands. "Bobbin what a very grown-up question you ask. You truly are special" and kissed her forehead and thought for a moment, then satisfied said quietly "Yule, my child is our woodland friend's most important season of the year. It celebrates the end of the old year bringing new light in the night, that's the full moon that comes just next week and the promise of new life coming for the woodland flowers and herbs, shrubs and all the trees. New life Bobbin is a wondrous time for all the animals of our wood, for in the Spring we will see new young life everywhere. That's why it's celebrated with family and friends."

Bobbin stood quietly smiling at Gigi and nodded her understanding, took her Great Grandmother by the hand and said, "Thank you Gigi, now I understand."

"Don't clean your teeth Bobbin until you've had your breakfast," said Gigi feeling tearful with her love for the child smiling up at her and put a tissue to her nose and sniffed.

"Why's that Gigi?" wondered Bobbin.

Gigi laughed "We'll have to start calling you Bobbin the Curious. It's because pancakes and honey are sweet and must be cleaned from our teeth when we've eaten them."

Bobbin opened the kitchen door and saw Grandad sitting at the kitchen table and ran up to him and threw her arms round his neck and kissed his cheek. "Good morning Grandad, I love you and Gigi so much."

Grandad returned her kiss and said, "These pancakes are delicious Bobbin."

"Sit down Bobbin these won't take a minute to cook," said Gigi as she poured her special Wildwood pancake mixture into a large flat pan. "I'm thinking my girl we'll make the Yule Cake this morning and finish your Yule Dress this afternoon. You and I have a busy day and Mummy and Daddy will want to speak to you later."

Bobbin looked at her Great Grandfather and asked "What are you doing today, Grandad?"

"I'm going up the lane to the farm and bringing back my donkey Juniper. He's going to carry the cake, a sack of Mistletoe I'm going to cut down from a tree I know, and also carry Gigi to the Fairy Wood tomorrow morning. Poor old Juniper, he's not as young as he was," replied Grandad. "It's a busy day for us all. But we love this time of year, don't we Gigi?"

....

"Put this apron on Bobbin," said Gigi, "and we'll make a start with our Wild Wood Cake."

Bobbin put the apron over her head and tied up the strings into a bow behind her back as she has seen her Mummy do a hundred times. "I'm so looking forward to helping you with this Gigi, just tell me what you want and I'll get it."

"Well," said Gigi getting her mixing spoons from the cupboard under the cutlery drawer and laying them in a row on the kitchen table, "for a start you can get me down that big mixing bowl," and pointed to a large bowl on the top shelf of the dresser.

Bobbin pulled a chair from the kitchen table and carried it to the dresser, climbed on it, then stretched up, took the bowl in one hand and stepped off the chair.

"Wow!" said a surprised Gigi, "I thought I would have to help you."

"No Gigi, my daddy says I'm strong just like him."

Gigi smiled and said, "Right, come with me into the larder."

Inside Gigi's big larder it was much cooler than the kitchen and an amazed Bobbin saw countless pots, jars, large wide bottles, bags and packages lining the three rows of shelves that reached almost to the larder's ceiling. On the lowest shelf were two large cardboard trays of eggs from Grandad's chickens that pecked and scratched in the shrubs and grasses under the trees close to the cottage. Beneath the shelves were bottles that were laid flat and stacked in special racks. There were sacks that were full of potatoes, turnips and parsnips, wooden trays brimming with carrots and the last of the summer tomatoes, still green waiting to be ripened in the winter's sun and, Grandad's favourite, Brussel sprouts still attached to their stalks waiting to be picked and cooked.

From the beams on the larder ceiling were hanging several bunches of wild aromatic herbs and onions, their long stalks platted together and hung from hooks and netting that held Wild Wood mushrooms and the even rarer truffles that Grandad's now ageing dog Bonny would find. These cold winter days Bonny would sleep, mostly nestled cosily on her cushion by the log burner and, when Grandad would ask her to come out with him, she would look at him with sleepy eyes, wag her tail once, put her head back on the cushion and close her eyes.

"What a lovely smell it is in here Gigi, with all these different smells mixed together, if I close my eyes, I think I'm in the Wild Wood," said the delighted Bobbin.

"That's exactly how I feel when I'm in here Bobbin. Now let's see what we have here," and looked closely at the middle shelf. "Ah yes, here we are," and Gigi took from the shelf a package labelled caster sugar and another even larger package labelled flour and gave them to Bobbin and said, "Put these on the kitchen table Bobbin." then reached behind another package and took a small tin box from its hiding place, fumbled in her apron's pocket and brought out her reading glasses, put them on her nose and looked at the box in her hand.

"That's what I'm looking for, Dark Cocoa Power. I knew it was up there," and gave it to Bobbin "Put that with the other ingredients and help me with the bottles of fruit, all picked by Grandad last summer in the Wild Wood."

....

The kitchen door opened and Gigi and Bobbin looked up from the mixing bowl, their aprons dusted with flour and caster sugar, their faces smeared with dark cocoa powder.

Grandad laughed at the sight of them both, "You two look as if you belong in the cake as well! Come and meet Juniper Bobbin," said Grandad, "Then I'll light the fire in the outside oven."

"Yes, Bobbin you go and see Juniper, I'll make a pot of tea. We both deserve a break then we'll pop the cake in the oven," said Gigi, filling a large iron kettle from the tap.

Juniper was tethered at the side of the cottage in the apple orchard nibbling hay from Grandad's shed he had put in a bag of rope netting and hung from one of the trees.

"Hello Juniper," said Bobbin "how are you? I've not seen you for weeks."

"My dear Miss Bobbin," replied Juniper "I am well, thank you and your Mummy and Daddy are well I hope?"

"Yes, thank you," she said.

"Oh Miss Bobbin, this hay Grandad keeps for me is so sweet and tasty," said Juniper and pulled another bunch of hay from the netting."

"Come on Bobbin, we must get that cake in the oven," said Grandad. "Juniper, I'll put you in the shed when you have finished the hay."

"Oh, I do love sleeping in Grandad's shed Miss Bobbin. It's so warm and comfortable," said Juniper taking another tuft of hay from the net, "I'll see you tomorrow."

The outside oven was at the back of the cottage behind the vegetable patch, sitting between the old greenhouse and Grandad's shed. It was an old iron cooking stove that was heated by lighting a fire in the firebox attached to the large cooking oven. It was here that every Yuletide Gigi would cook her Wild Wood Cake.

Grandad opened the kitchen door. "When you're ready Gigi I've got my wheelbarrow here."

Gigi had just finished pouring the cake mixture into a large baking tin and Bobbin asked giggling, "Why do we need a wheelbarrow?"

"It does seem odd doesn't it," laughed Gigi, "but I don't know what we'd do without Grandad's wheelbarrow at Yule and for the Wild Wood stews I make in the dark days of deep midwinter. Reynard and the badger brothers Bardon and Blade love my stews."

Grandad picked up the cake tin and put it into his wheelbarrow and walked up the garden towards the vegetable patch with Bobbin and Gigi following.

The oven was hot and the fire burning brightly with extra logs stacked against the oven drying off after the night's frost.

Grandad opened the oven door and put the cake mixture inside and quickly closed the door, "Keeping the heat in," he said to Bobbin, "that'll take, oh what Gigi, about three hours to cook?"

"About that Grandad," answered Gigi. "I'll have a look at it anyway in about two hours though," and looked over Grandad's shoulder and pointed: "There's little Burnet, let's see what he's here for."

"Hello Gigi, hello Grandad, oh hello Miss Bobbin," said Burnet the Little Owl, "Are you all well? It's a lovely day don't you think Miss Bobbin? How are your parents, I hope they are well also?"

Bobbin smiled to herself and greeted Burnet patiently and waited for him to come to the point of his visit.

Grandad stepped forward smiling at the Little Owl. "We are all well thank you Burnet. Do you have a message for us by any chance?"

The Little Owl looked startled. "Oh yes, I nearly forgot," he giggled. "My cousin Alfred sends his greetings and asks me to inform you that tomorrow morning, Yule that is, Oberon with be here to escort you to the Oak Wood. Oh, and that scallywag fox will be with him, the Lord Devon wanted an escort for Oberon" and put his wing up to his mouth. "Oh I forgot, I mustn't call that fox a scallywag any more. Lord Devon says we must now call him by his name only, Reynard that is." He pulled a funny face at Bobbin and said "That's until he spoils himself again of course." He laughed.

....

It was late afternoon and the sky darkening, for tomorrow was Yule in the Wild Wood and the High Moor, where birds and the animals alike were eagerly preparing themselves for the festival in the Oak Wood, where the Fairies lived.

The Fairies had finished gathering and cooking all the woodland food that was to be eaten at their Yule feast and had rested in their neat and cosy hidden homes, some inside the trunks of ancient trees, others in warm dry caves in the rocky bank that rose onto the High Moor.

The queen of the Fairies, Celandine, whose name in flower language means *the joy yet come*, lived with her consort Herb-Robert and their fairy children in a huge Yew tree at the centre of the Oak Wood. The Yew tree, it seemed to Alfred and Grandad really not belonging there, for it was so obviously out of place, standing among the huge ancient oaks.

This unusual, out of place Yew had stood there before the Oaks. The squirrels had hidden acorns from a nearby oak wood near the Yew, to eat in the wintertime when other food became scarce. Alfred told Grandad that he believed the acorns that had not been eaten had seeded and grown into the Oak Wood it was today. The Yew, Alfred thought was much older than the Oaks and had stood in the centre of what was once a sacred grove, a shrine for the ancient people and animals that once had lived and farmed this blessed land.

Herb-Robert, despite his sinister flower name, was a jolly, likable consort to Queen Celandine. He was bigger and more robust than other fairies and his queen had made him guardian of her Oak Wood and all those that lived there. He would three times daily patrol the borders of the wood warning and shooing off any intruding weasel and stoat on the ground and any rook or crow that flew in the air from the High Moor with his long Yew fighting staff.

Should the scallywags from the High Moor, especially Mouse Ear and Larkspur, become too much for the bold Herb-Robert he would seek Alfred the Owl's wise council and the Lord Devon's and lately young Oberon's fearsome antlers.

Both Queen Celandine and her Consort knew how lucky they and all their large extended fairy family were to be living next to the Wild Wood, for the animals that lived there were their friends who would care for them in difficult times. Especially in the coming weeks of deepest winter when Grandad and Gigi would bring hot Winter Stews and cake for the children. All of them were now excitedly looking forward to meeting the new and special person into their lives, for they knew Miss Bobbin was about to become their own very special friend.

....

Bobbin stood in front of Gigi's full-length mirror that stood in an empty corner of Gigi's and Grandad's bedroom. She was dressed in the Yule dress and cloak Gigi had just finished, and standing back with a critical eye Gigi adjusted the cloak, pulling the hood over Bobbin's head then stepping back again. "The dress is not too tight, is it Bobbin?" she asked. "This time next year I'll have to let it out a bit. What do you think of it? Are you comfortable in it my precious?"

Bobbin looked at herself in the mirror seeing her dress of Forest Green made from boiled wool and covered with moons in all their phases, stars from the night sky, leaping hares with long ears and owls, Wood Owls, Barn Owls, Long Eared Owls and of course Little Owls. There were Red Deer standing proud with fully grown antlers, foxes, badgers and another smaller symbol over her heart she did not recognise and turned round quickly to Gigi, delighting in the way her dress and cloak swirled out gracefully.

"Gigi, what does this mean?" Bobbin asked pointing to her heart.

"Take the cloak off Bobbin I have to finish sewing on our favourite animals we know from the Wild Wood," said Gigi. "That's Brigid to us country folk, others will call her Saint Brigid, but not us, we know who she is," she answered seriously "She, Bobbin, is our Goddess of healing, poetry and the fire of the sun and the earth, the fertility of the land and its people and animals. She is our very special Goddess who cares for us all. Come on let's go downstairs and I'll finish your cloak in front of the fire, your Mummy and Daddy will be calling soon."

....

There was a thick frost on the windows of Bobbin's bedroom and the glass was sparkling in the moonlight for just the other side of the window pane the air was freezing, the night still dark in spite of the moon's new quarter and a frozen stillness in Grandad's garden and the Wild Wood beyond. The chickens, now all in their hutch were sleeping comfortably on their perches. Juniper in Grandad's shed had eaten his fill of hay and was asleep on a soft warm pile of straw Gigi had laid for him. It seemed nothing was moving, no one awake, the garden and the Wild Wood, silent and at peace with themselves.

"Well!" said an irritated Reynard noisily, "Grandad hasn't even got the kitchen light on yet. I knew you got me out of bed too early Oberon."

The chickens in their hutch were startled awake and clucked and crowed, Juniper the donkey brayed loudly in protest as donkeys do when suddenly disturbed from their sleep. Even worse, Reynard had alarmed the pigeons that roosted in the trees tops round Grandad's cottage who took to flight, their collective wings making a sharp flapping sound that wakened other birds sleeping on the lower branches of the trees.

Oberon looked down at Reynard, an impatient expression on his young handsome face. "You really are a silly fox aren't you Reynard," he said quietly and Reynard now realising what he had done dropped his head in shame. "Try thinking first before you shout something. I shall tell Grandad it was you that woke everyone up."

"What have I done wrong," pleaded Reynard. "I only said Grandad was still asleep. Tell me, what have I done wrong?" and stood up on his hind legs in protest.

"Get down you silly fox and behave yourself. Do you want me to tell my father?" said the amused Oberon lowering his now fully grown antlers and shaking them at the fox.

Reynard jumped back startled, "I'll tell Alfred if you whack me Oberon."

"Stop being silly Reynard. Look! Grandad's kitchen light has come on, look what you have done now, you have woken Grandad up as well!" as the cottage's kitchen door opened and Grandad himself stepped out.

"I see you Oberon and you Reynard, stop squabbling, you're waking the whole Wild Wood. Come to the cottage and I'll get you some fresh water and some nice, sweet hay for you Oberon and a bowl of Gigi's stew for you Reynard," then shook his head and smiled at them both.

"There," said Reynard, "Grandad isn't angry with me, I told you it wasn't my fault," and gave one of his silly grins at Oberon.

"Grandad is too nice to Tell you Off, you silly fox," responded Oberon, laughing at Reynard.

"Will you two, stop arguing," said Burnet quietly from a branch just over their heads. "And if you, Reynard, don't behave yourself, I'll tell Alfred."

....

"A Joyous Yule!" called Burnet as Bobbin stepped out from the kitchen door dressed in her Yule dress, her cloak and hood that kept her from feeling the winter morning's chill, woollen gloves to keep her fingers warm and her strong winter boots to keep her feet warm and dry. She was carrying two wreathes of platted Mistletoe and Holly with its bright winter berries.

Startled, Bobbin looked up and saw Burnet wave a wing at her, she waved back and called "Happy Yule Burnet, are you coming with us?"

"Yes Miss Bobbin, Alfred wants me to fly ahead and tell him when you reach the Secret Lake. Isn't it all so exciting," said Burnet eagerly.

"Hello Burnet," called Grandad carrying the tin of Yuletide cake, "Did Alfred tell you to keep an eye on those two?" and looked over at Oberon and Reynard.

"Well really Grandad, he's such a silly fox you know," said Burnet looking down at Reynard who was pulling faces and poking out his tongue at Oberon who was half-heartedly shaking his antler at the silly fox and laughing.

"Well," said Grandad, "you won't get Oberon complaining, he likes Reynard too much and enjoys his company. Anyway, I have to get Juniper from my shed" and walked off into the garden.

Gigi arrived dressed in her Yule clothing and cloak, a black felt wool pointed hat and wellington boots. She put a small wreath of mistletoe over the hood of Bobbin's cloak, stood back then adjusted it to sit more comfortably on her head, put another over her pointed hat and said looking at the wreathes Bobbin was holding. "Put one on Oberon's antlers and the other round Reynard's neck" and looked over at them both. "Joyous Yule to you both my dears and behave yourselves. I heard you arguing" and smiled at them both.

Bobbin walked over to Oberon who greeted her shyly. "Joyous Yule Miss Bobbin. My mother is waiting for you at the Oak Wood"

"Joyous Yule dear Oberon," said Bobbin and gently placed the Mistletoe and Holly wreath on Oberon's antlers.

Then she turned to Reynard. "Joyous Yule my dear Reynard. How is your leg now?" and placed the smaller wreath over Reynard's head resting round his neck.

"Joyous Yule Miss Bobbin, my leg still hurts a little. Oberon walks so fast you know," said Reynard, holding his once-injured leg up for Bobbin to see.

"Oh, do shut up you silly fox," called Oberon impatiently.

"You can't call me that, your father said...," complained Reynard.

"Be quiet! Both of you," said the Little Owl, "Or I will tell Alfred!"

Grandad arrived back at the kitchen door with Juniper and a large hessian sack full of mistletoe which was tied to the saddle over juniper's back. "Up you get Gigi and I'll tie the cake tin on the back of the saddle behind you," then he called to Bobbin, Oberon and Reynard "Off you go, don't walk too fast, Juniper will get tired." He closed the kitchen door and took Juniper's halter and walked up the garden path and into the Wild Wood.

As the forest trees closed in around them Grandad softly called to the tree tops, "Joyous Yule Cernunnos on this happy day."

Bobbin whispered to Oberon, "Who's Cernunnos."

Oberon replied in a hushed voice, "The Green Man, he's our God of the Wild Wood, the High Moor and all the surrounding countryside."

....

At the Secret Lake, Hernshaw the Heron and Moonbeam the Otter were waiting. Hernshaw was at the far edge of the lake by the Sacred Grove, for behind the Grove was a secret path that led to the Oak Wood and used only at special times of the year. At Yule time Grandad and Gigi with Juniper would use this path as honoured guests of the fairies, but today the Fairy Queen Celandine had told the Lord Devon to bring Bobbin to the Oak Wood by way of the hidden Sacred Grove path, escorted by two of his trusted friends. And so, Lord Devon had instructed his councillor Alfred to arrange for Hernshaw to meet them at the Secret Lake and for

Moonbeam to race to the Oak Wood and tell Queen Celandine when they reached the hidden path.

Hernshaw had told Moonbeam to wait at the other side of the Lake for Grandad and his family to arrive then tell them to meet him at the Sacred Grove.

The Otter had become bored waiting for Grandad's party and began to play. First diving to the bottom of the lake and finding river clams and throwing them towards Hernshaw laughing and clapping his paws together, then rummaging and splashing through the remains of the summer's Bulrushes and chasing out the ducks and moorhens, then turning on his back and swimming after them.

"Hello, hello," called Hernshaw from across the lake "you silly Otter. I can see Miss Bobbin with Oberon and that scally..... I mean Reynard. They are almost at the Lake. Get back there and meet them!" Hernshaw felt he should be cross with Moonbeam but could not find his anger and just shook his head, for he loved his silly Otter friend dearly.

"Moonbeam," called Bobbin, "Joyous Yule" and as she got closer to the Otter she asked, "Moonbeam what's all those leaves on your coat?" and pointed. "And there's a bulrush stalk stuck behind your ear"

Moonbeam grinned "I've been chasing the ducks Miss Bobbin" and sat up and held his paws out in greeting and then giggled.

"More like chasing his tail I would think Miss Bobbin," offered Reynard and smiled at his own joke.

"Don't be unkind now Reynard," said Bobbin gently.

"Yes," said Oberon, "shut up Reynard."

"I only said he was chasing....," said Reynard turning to Oberon.

"Are you two still arguing!" said Grandad, trying to hide his amusement.

Both Oberon and Reynard gave each other a playful look and Reynard stuck his tongue out and Oberon shook his antlers as Bobbin walked over to Moonbeam and asked, "Are you here to meet us?" and felt Grandad softly place his hand on her shoulder.

"Oh yes Miss Bobbin," said the giggling Otter. "Hello Grandad, Joyous Yule to you both, I hope you are both well."

Grandad and Bobbin looked up over Moonbeam's head as they heard Hernshaw's call, "Get on with it you silly Otter!"

Moonbeam stopped giggling and said seriously, "I am to tell you Grandad to meet Hernshaw at the Sacred Grove" and pointed a paw across the lake.

Grandad said his thanks to Moonbeam and told Oberon and Reynard to continue and said to Bobbin, "See they both behave themselves" and smiled and winked at his Great Grand Daughter.

Hernshaw was waiting at the grove's altar as the party arrived and greeted them all formally and wishing them a Joyous Yule, then spoke to Grandad directly: "Grandad, I am told by Alfred who was commanded by Queen Celandine to tell you and especially Miss Bobbin" and lowered his head in respect "that you, Miss Bobbin and of course Gigi and Juniper are to use the Secret Path into the Oak Wood."

"Thank you Hernshaw we will," spoke Grandad, just as formally as Hernshaw had spoken. "Can I ask if my friends and escort can come with us?" and gave Hernshaw a wink of his eye that only the Heron would see.

"Only if they both behave themselves Grandad," replied Hernshaw with a twinkle in his eyes, then turned and called to Flash the Kingfisher who had been watching from a branch of a tree that hung over the lake.

Flash flew to Hernshaw and hovered over his head. "I know, I'm to fly to the Oak Wood and tell Alfred that Grandad, Miss Bobbin with Gigi are now on the Secret Path. Is that right?"

"With Juniper and their escorts," corrected Hernshaw.

"Oh yes, oh here comes that silly Otter. I'm not speaking to him Hernshaw, he's still taking my fish!"

"Off you go then Flash" and turned his eyes to the sky impatiently.

"I thought I was taking that message to Alfred," said a disappointed Moonbeam.

"Oh, do be quiet you silly Otter," replied an exasperated Hernshaw. "We'll see them all shortly in the Oak Wood, besides Flash is faster than you are, as I have told you before."

....

"This is a great honour for us Bobbin and for Oberon and Reynard, especially for Oberon as it acknowledges he will one day take on his father's mantle of responsibility for all this land" and winked at Bobbin. "And for Reynard it also acknowledges the trust Lord Devon and Queen Celandine have in him."

Reynard the Fox stopped and looked round at Grandad, grinned then stuck his nose in the air and continued very sedately down the Secret Path.

"Reynard," called Oberon, "your nose is in the air again, you silly fox."

"No, it's not, you silly Red Deer," said Reynard, "This is how I always walk."

"Behave yourselves you two," said Grandad, "or I will tell Alfred" and grinned at Bobbin, who smiled back.

"Is that singing I can hear?" called Gigi, seated comfortably on the back of Juniper the donkey.

"Yes, it is," said Grandad, "the fairies and the Wild Wood folk are singing Yule Carols, how wonderful. Can you hear them, Bobbin?"

"Yes, I can. But I can't make out the words," replied Bobbin.

"Oh, I know this carol" and Gigi began to sing in her rich natural voice:

"The holly and the ivy
in the Wild Wood side by side
There the Lady and the antlered one
are together in the winter's blight.
The feeding of the bright fire
and the dancing by its light.
The singing of the Yuletide carols
to celebrate this night."

Bobbin looked at her Great Grand Mother in wonder. "That is lovely Gigi, would you teach me those songs?"

"You'll know them by heart at the end of the day, we'll be singing them one after another," said Gigi. "I think I'll get down now Grandad and walk the rest of the way, we're nearly there."

....

The Secret Path led them into the Oak Wood and as they stepped off the path, they heard what must have been a hundred voices singing. Then they entered into what appeared to them a huge cathedral of trees all dressed in swathes of holly, red berries and masses of Ivy. They walked further into the Oak Wood and saw in the centre of this multi-shaded green and brown living edifice, a large bonfire burning brightly, fed by great logs from fallen trees spreading the fire's warmth throughout this verdant mansion. The surrounding oak tree's great trunks were the pillars of this palace, giving support to the roof of thick branches above their heads. The Oaks' lower thick strong branches were the flying buttresses that supported the pillars.

The Yew was the far side of the fire where a Cathedral's High Altar would be. In front of the Yew altar sat Queen Celandine, gracefully dressed in all her majestic and magical gossamer silkiness, holding a simple Yew wand decorated with Holly leaves, their red winter berries and Ivy, a powerful, although understated symbol of her authority and magical power.

Standing behind the throne to Queen Celandine's right, his head and huge antlers held high, stood the majestic Lord Devon himself. To her left stood Herb-Robert her consort, who was wearing a forest green worsted jacket that reached down to his knees and secured by a large leather belt.

Herb-Robert's leggings were of the same material as his jacket, but in a much darker green, while his knee-length boots were made of the finest felt. He stood next to his queen, legs apart, in his right hand his Yew Fighting Pole, one end resting on the ground next to his right foot and gripping the pole just above his waist. This display of power and authority sent reassuring messages to the Fairy folk and all the Wild Wood animals and birds watching. It certainly sent shivers down the spines of Mouse Ear and Larkspur who were hidden high in a tree determined to see the fairy spectacle they had heard about since children but never been allowed to see.

Queen Celandine's throne was made entirely of Royal Stag antlers that came from a long line of ancestors of the Lord Devon and skilfully made into the throne by the Queen's fairy craftsmen. The throne was draped with the feathers of dozens of swans that lived on the Secret Lake and the rivers of the High Moor who would bring them to her in the summertime when they had finished moulting.

She rested on great cushions made from silk harvested from the silk worms that lived in the oak wood and fine linen and cotton that had been woven and spun from plants all over the two woods and the High Moor that were grown by her gardeners then stuffed with down given by the ducks that lived in the surrounding countryside. It was a wondrous throne that shimmered in the gentle breezes blowing through the Oak Wood that rustled the feathers as the great cushions glinted and sparkled in the light from the bright fire.

Grandad and Gigi took Bobbin's hands in theirs and slowly walked round the fire and stopped and waited for the Queen to see them.

The Queen had been speaking with the Lord Devon and her consort when Herb-Robert saw Grandad, Gigi and Bobbin approach and spoke to his Queen. She immediately turned and smiled, calling them forward to her presence.

Bobbin was wide-eyed in wonder, awestruck by the beauty of the magical scene before her and stepped forward gingerly, holding both Grandad's and Gigi's hands.

Celandine stood and slowly stepped down from her throne and walked up to them smiling a warm greeting "Grandad and Gigi I am so happy you are both here again to celebrate with us on this Yuletide. You are both my honoured guests and companions."

Bobbin gripped both Grandad's and Gigi's hands tighter, overwhelmed by the Queen's glowing beauty and the soft melodious tones of her voice.

The Queen's gaze settled on Bobbin who instantly released her hands from Grandad and Gigi putting her hands to her side and stood straight, head up and looked at Queen Celandine directly, her face serious to the occasion.

The Queen smiled at Bobbin, "Come to me my dear child" and held out her hands.

Bobbin stepped forward not knowing where her courage was coming from. It was something she knew instinctively she would do. "My name is Celandine. You and I will call each other by our given names child" and held Bobbin's face in her hands and said, "You and I dearest Bobbin are going to be special friends and as we grow older, we shall become closer friends. I am so pleased to have you with me this day. We shall speak later for I have something special to say to you" and turned away going back to her throne as Bobbin returned to her Great Grand Parents.

"Did you hear what the Queen said to me Grandad?" asked the bewildered Bobbin.

"Yes, Bobbin we did and so did everyone else, for when the Queen speaks, magically all hear," said Grandad, smiling at Gigi.

Oberon came to them and announced, "Grandad, Gigi, Miss Bobbin your seating is over there" and pointed to a fallen tree trunk draped in linen and cushions to relax on "near the fire. Herb-Robert is fetching some refreshments for you" and turned to Bobbin, "Miss Bobbin, my mother would like your company, she's over there."

Bobbin looked over to the side of the Yew and saw Titania standing among all the Wild Wood animals and birds that Bobbin had come to know and love since her first visit to wood with Grandad.

Titania saw Bobbin and lifted her head in greeting as Bobbin saw her and waved excitedly and both came together in a rush, Titania laying her head on Bobbin's shoulder and Bobbin hugging Titania's neck.

"Dear Lady Titania, I have missed you these last few days," said Bobbin tearfully. "May I wish you and your family a Joyous Yule."

"My dearest Miss Bobbin, I wish you and your Mummy and Daddy a Joyous Yule. And you and I have no need to be so formal, Bobbin." Titania smiled playfully.

"Of course, Titania," replied Bobbin, gently laughing and looking over at her other Wild Wood friends. "Would you come with me to greet my friends over there?" as everyone round the fire began to sing once more.

"Silent night, Solstice night
all is calm, all is bright.
Nature slumbers in forest and glade
While snowflakes blanket the sleeping earth
as Yule fires welcome the sun's rebirth, see
the light reborn.
See the light return.

Bobbin first came upon Hernshaw the Heron and his friend Moonbeam the Otter. "Hello, you both, I am so very pleased to see you and a Joyous Yule."

"Joyous Yule Miss Bobbin," said Hernshaw formally, standing upright and proud the way all herons hold themselves.

While Moonbeam giggled and clapped his paws together, "Joyous Yule Miss Bobbin. Did you see me chasing the ducks?"

Hernshaw tutted, "Be quiet you silly otter. Miss Bobbin, would you say hello to my cousin Patience who lives on the High Moor?"

Bobbin looked over Hernshaw and saw another heron who said "Hello Miss Bobbin, a Joyous Yule. I am very pleased to meet you. Hernshaw has told me all about you. Would you visit me on the High Moor next summer? I would be very pleased to see you."

"I would love to," said Bobbin. "I will ask Hernshaw and Moonbeam to show me the way."

"Miss Bobbin, Miss Bobbin" called Bardon and Blade the badger brothers, "a Joyous Yule Miss Bobbin" and stood upright on their hind legs and waved to her.

"Hello, you two," called Bobbin, "A Joyous Yule to you two as well. I love your mistletoe wreaths they really suit you both."

Titania gently nudged Bobbin. "Bobbin, my Lord Devon would wish you well, he's standing behind Queen Celandine."

The great stag turned as Bobbin approached and raised his Antlers in a majestic greeting, "Joyous Yule Miss Bobbin" and approached her and laid his head gently on her shoulder.

Bobbin placed her arms round the stags great neck briefly then stepped back and formally said "Joyous Yule Lord Devon"

"My dear child between you and my family, there shall be no formality. You are a part of the Wild Wood now," said Lord Devon. "Greet the rest of your friends then return here, the Queen wishes to speak to you before it grows dark. There is Alfred" and pointed with his antlers, "Go and wish him a Joyous Yule, he would be so happy to hear that from you."

Bobbin looked up and saw Alfred the Owl perched on a low branch of the Yew tree just behind Herb-Robert and waved. "Alfred," she called quietly and went over to him, "Joyous Yule dearest Alfred," she said in a hushed voice. "We haven't spoken for some days. I miss you tapping on my bedroom window."

Alfred opened his wings in greeting and hopped to a lower branch. "My dear Miss Bobbin a Joyous Yule to you and your Mummy and Daddy" and dropped to an even lower branch where he and Bobbin were at last looking at each other face to face. "That's better. But you know Miss Bobbin every night when you are at home with Mummy and Daddy I fly over your house and now I land on your bedroom window ledge and look through the window at you sleeping in your bed" and raised his wings again to emphasise the importance of what he had just said. "But don't tell Mummy or Daddy, they'll think it odd behaviour."

"Thank you, dear Alfred," said Bobbin, "It is very comforting to know you are close by in the night. I wish I could tell Mummy and Daddy about you."

"One day dearest Miss Bobbin, one day. But they must understand your secret first. One day though," said Alfred. "Oh, here's young Burnet."

"A Joyous Yule Miss Bobbin, I hope your Mummy and Daddy are well," said Burnet eagerly. "Oh, and Gigi says don't spend too much time away from the fire or you'll get cold. I must fly" and flew off.

"Before you go Miss Bobbin come and speak to Talon the Crow, he will look after you when you visit Patience the Heron next summer. He is our friend now all that nonsense is over," said Alfred. "Come with me Miss Bobbin" and flew to another tree just behind where Grandad and Gigi were sitting.

"Talon, Talon come down and speak to Miss Bobbin," called Alfred and seemingly out of nowhere a great black bird dropped onto the branch Alfred was sitting on.

Talon's appearance took Bobbin by surprise and she quickly stepped back and gasped.

"Oh dear, Miss Bobbin I am dreadfully sorry to have startled you. Please forgive me," said Talon dropping his head in shame.

"I should think so Talon for I am Miss Bobbin's escort for the day," said Reynard suddenly appearing.

Bobbin collected herself and said to Talon "Please don't apologise Talon, you took me by surprise that's all. I am here to wish you and your family a Joyous Yule and hope to see you next summer when I visit Patience the Heron on the High Moor."

"I shall look forward to that Miss Bobbin and be honoured to escort you when you arrive," said Talon dropping his head once more in a sign of respect. "Joyous Yule Miss Bobbin" and dropped his head again shyly.

"I should be your escort Miss Bobbin," said Reynard irritably.

Bobbin reached down and gently scratched Reynard on the top of his head, "You shall both be my escorts," said Bobbin and smiled her special smile at Talon who dropped his head again.

"I can see you up there you two!" called Alfred looking up into the Oak. "Come down here at once!"

There was a silence, no movement, no sound of voices as Bobbin and Reynard gazed up into the tree wondering who it was up there.

"You two had better get down here," called Talon angrily.

Bobbin and Reynard heard two small voices arguing and the sound of rustling as whoever it was began to climb down from the tree top.

"You had better hurry!" called Reynard.

"Shoosh!" said Alfred, "You silly fox."

Bobbin stroked the back of Reynard's head as Larkspur the Stoat and Mouse Ear the Weasel both appeared at the bottom of the tree.

"You were both told by the Lord Devon not to come to the Oak Wood again," said Alfred seriously.

Both Larkspur and Mouse Ear opened their mouths and began moving their lips while thinking what they could say to Alfred. Then as soon as Larkspur began speaking Mouse Ear repeated his friend's words, both working themselves into a frenzy of excitement.

"Yes no," said Larkspur, "No yes," said Mouse Ear nudging Larkspur with his elbow.

"Do be quiet you two," ordered Alfred putting a wing across his face to hide his laughter.

"Well, it wasn't my fault," whined Mouse Ear.

"Yes it was, you suggested we go and watch the celebration," gasped Larkspur to his friend.

"We were only watching, Alfred. Larkspur said you wouldn't see us high in the tree top," said Mouse Ear in desperation.

"I said no such thing Mouse Ear. I didn't Alfred. We are so sorry though," said Larkspur hesitantly.

"Yes Alfred, we are so sorry," said the wide-eyed Mouse Ear.

Alfred looked at Talon who said, "I saw them Alfred and was about to send them away when you arrived."

Alfred replied with a smile at his new friend Talon. "They are really such silly folk from the High Moor, but it's Yule so let's be forgiving at this time" and turned to Larkspur and Mouse Ear who were now holding each other and gazing at Alfred wide-eyed. "You two come and sit on this branch and make sure no one else sees you and I'll ask Miss Bobbin to arrange for a piece of Gigi's Yule cake to be brought to you."

Both Larkspur and Mouse Ear first looked at each other in amazement, then gave each other a silly lopsided grin and scampered up the tree and found a hiding place in the shadows next to the trunk as singing began once more.

Away in a manger, so warm in Grandad's shed
the little Lord Devon laid down his sweet head.
The stars in the bright sky looked down where he lay.
The little Lord Devon, asleep on the hay.
The deer herd were lowing, the fawn awakes
The little Lord Devon no crying he makes.
We love you Lord Devon, look up at the sky
and stay by our side 'till morning is nigh.

Alfred whispered in Bobbin's ear, "That is the fairy carol to our Lord Devon, isn't it wonderful Miss Bobbin"
"It is Alfred," said Bobbin and looked over at Lord Devon, his great antlers raised up majestically.
"And look at Queen Celandine," spoke Alfred quietly.
Bobbin who had put her arms again round Oberon's shoulders looked at the Fairy Queen who was now stood up and facing Lord Devon and singing heartedly with all the other fairies and the folk from the Wild Wood.
Alfred gently nudged Bobbin and pointed over at the stoat and weasel from the High Moor. "What silly folk they are, I don't know why we all took them so seriously when they said they would spoil this celebration."
Bobbin looked over at Larkspur and Mouse Ear once more to see them holding each other's paws and trying to sing the song they did not know and she giggled her delight.

"Now you and the Lady Titania go and sit with Grandad and Gigi and get warm," said Alfred, "and oh, don't forget to speak to Flash the Kingfisher, he's a great admirer of yours Miss Bobbin."

"Thank you, Alfred," answered Bobbin, "I will" and said to Titania, "Would you sit with me by Grandad and Gigi for a while? I'm beginning to feel quite cold."

Titania smiled at her and said, "I would love to it's been a while since Gigi and I have spoken."

....

Flash the Kingfisher appeared hovering at Bobbin's side, "Joyous Yule Miss Bobbin. We all love your dress and cloak. Did Gigi make it for you?"

"Yes, she did Flash, thank you, I love it also, it's so warm," said Bobbin. "Have you had some of Gigi's Yule cake?

"We all have Miss Bobbin, we love Gigi's Yule cake and Bardon and Blade are now serving second helpings to those not yet full up!" and laughed excitedly. "By the way Miss Bobbin, Alfred has asked if you would speak to the Queen again as you will be leaving shortly before it gets too dark."

Bobbin turned to the Lady Titania and told her she was to see the Queen again and Titania replied, "Dear Bobbin let's see each other soon, my son Oberon will guide you back to Grandad's cottage" and laid her head gently on Bobbin's shoulder.

Grandad looked over as Bobbin stood to go and said "Don't be long Bobbin we must leave shortly to get back to the cottage before dark."

....

The Fairy Queen Celandine took both of Bobbin's hands in hers and looked directly into her eyes. "My dearest Bobbin, you and I will see each other in the springtime unless I need your help in the deep midwinter. There is something sacred I must say to you before you leave here, let us sit.

The Queen returned to her throne and Bobbin was shown to a seat next to her by Herb-Robert who whispered, "We are all looking forward to seeing you again soon Miss Bobbin."

Queen Celandine leaned forward and took her hand and said in her regal voice that everyone in the Fairy Wood could hear, "The thirteen goals for your future life Bobbin are:

Known yourself
Know your craft
Learn and grow
Apply knowledge with wisdom
Achieve balance
Keep your words in good order
Keep your thoughts in good order
Celebrate life
Attune with the cycles of the earth
Breath and eat correctly
Exercise the body
Meditate
Honour the Gods and Goddesses of this land"

"Go in peace my child, said Queen Celandine" and kissed her on her cheek.

Bobbin stood from the seat, turned and stepped into the arms of Grandad who wrapped his arms round her and led her back to Gigi who was mounting Juniper. "Would you like to sit with me on Juniper Bobbin?"

"Thank you Gigi, but can I walk with Oberon and Reynard?" asked Bobbin kissing Titania on her forehead.

"Of course, my lovely one and put your hood up, it grows cold," called Gigi as Grandad led Juniper out of the Oak Wood to the Secret Path back to the Secret Lake and on to the cottage as Bobbin remembered it was Christmas Eve and her Mummy and Daddy would be there in the morning.

Deep Midwinter

"Hello Miss Bobbin" called the Robin.

Bobbin's Mummy and Daddy had just dropped her off at Gigi and Grandad's front garden with their family dog Manu, kissed them both and Daddy sounded his horn letting Gigi and Grandad know Bobbin had arrived.

Bobbin and Manu were inseparable when at home together and both pleased they would have some time together with Gigi and Grandad while their parents were away for few days on their mid-January shopping trip to London. Especially as they always had a present for them when they arrived home.

It was Grandad who had chosen Manu for his Grandson James, Bobbin's father a few months before Sophie had given birth to their daughter. Manu, although still a pup himself had immediately taken on the role of her guard and had watched over her ever since. Just as both Grandad and Gigi secretly knew Manu would.

The air was freezing, full of a dank wet mist that had risen from the Secret Lake during the night. The moisture in the mist had frozen on the trees of the Wild Wood leaving the whole wood covered in a deceptively beguiling hoar frost. It had snowed briefly over the New Year leaving the frozen ground slippery and hard. Although now the older and wiser woodland animals and birds were saying it was too cold to snow, this week anyway. But they touched their hearts asking the Goddess Brigit to see any snowfall was not too deep.

Already the Deep Mid-Winter had begun to reach out its icy fingers to touch the woodlanders and the High Moor folk, slowly tightening its freezing grip on the lives of all that lived and sheltered there.

The ground, grasses, plants and bushes were covered in what looked to Bobbin to be Gigi's icing sugar they had used on the Yule cake. The branches of the woodland trees were thick with the crystalline covering that sparkled ominously in the misty winter's wan sunlight, for the frigid mid-winter frosts were a danger to all those that lived in the Wild Wood and on the High Moor.

It was cold, very cold and Bobbin knew instinctively that she needed to visit her woodland friends, especially Queen Celandine's family and friends, fleetingly having an impression that Queen Celandine was calling to her.

Now beginning to worry for her fairy friends, the frowning Bobbin looked up and saw the Robin Redbreast perched on Grandad's garden gate and smiled "Hello Ruddock, lovely to see you again so soon. Aren't you cold?" she asked, knowing she must tell Grandad and Gigi of her thoughts as soon as she saw them.

"Oh no Miss Bobbin, I have a nice cosy winter nest in a hole of an oak with the rest of my family, and there is still food to eat if you know where to find it of course, and especially with what Gigi and Grandad put out for us." He paused thinking, "But there are some birds not as robust as I and my family are that will suffer dreadfully if we don't take care of them and some animals as well," said the Robin with worried eyes. "Are you here to help them Miss Bobbin?"

Bobbin looked at Ruddock the Robin and answering thoughtfully replied, "Do you know, I believe I am."

Manu, who had been listening to Bobbin and Ruddock, looked up at his beloved Bobbin with wonder in his eyes. "Bobbin," he said, "you and I have been speaking together since the day you were born and I never knew you could speak to other animals."

"It's a secret Manu, you mustn't tell anyone else. Only Gigi and Grandad know," whispered Bobbin. "I didn't know myself until they showed me I could" and brushed her hand lovingly over Manu's head and spoke to the Robin:

"Ruddock, would you tell Alfred that Grandad and I are coming to the Wild Wood with a bowl of Gigi's stew and rich fruits of the forest winter cake please," said Bobbin. She thought for a moment and added, "And to ask if I could visit with Queen Celandine, I think she is wanting to see me."

"I will Miss Bobbin," said Ruddock, "Goodbye for now and you Manu" and flitted off towards the frozen Wild Wood.

Manu wagged his tail and gave a low "Woof" as Bobbin wrapped her coat more tightly round herself and adjusted her bobble hat and looked over at Grandad's frost-covered gardens, the apple orchard and the tall trees of the Wild Wood beyond.

The picture that came to her from somewhere deep in her mind's eye was of an unrecognisable starkness, a frozen grimness and all the more dangerous to her animal and bird friends.

The deceptive beauty of this picturesque scene gave a dangerous complacency to the unwitting, the careless and the foolish, as a familiar little voice in her head whispered, "Take care Bobbin beware the Wild Wood's winter's night."

The cottage door opened and Gigi called, "Bobbin! Manu! Come inside, it's freezing."

"Hello Gigi," shouted Bobbin delightfully and ran up the path and into her Great Grandmother's arms.

"Come inside my precious and let's get those cold clothes off you quickly," said Gigi, happy to have her Bobbin with her once more. "Hello Manu, I'll get you some water and a bone to chew. Go and say hello to Bonny, she's sleeping as usual in the kitchen."

"Where's Grandad Gigi? I feel that Queen Celandine needs to speak with me," spoke Bobbin, a worried look in her eyes.

Gigi took Bobbin in her arms and kissed the top of her head, then held her at arm's length. "Now Bobbin," said Gigi seriously, "Don't worry your little head about our woodland friends, Grandad and I look after them every year at this time" and frowned. "The Queen must be worried to call you though, usually when she sends us a message it's because the fairies are running short of firewood" and looked out of the kitchen window. "Oh, Grandad's speaking with Alfred, why don't you go and tell them?"

Bobbin pulled her bobble hat back on and ran out of the kitchen door, down the path to the bottom of the garden with Manu on her heels and, there at the gate that led into the Wild Wood, stood Grandad, wearing his winter storm coat and felt hat, speaking with Alfred the Owl.

Grandad and Alfred heard them both running down the path towards them, Bobbin running excitedly with Manu just behind her, his floppy ears bouncing up and down in time with his leaping run, his long silky hair streaming out from his body and shining in the morning's sunlight.

"This must be all very important Bobbin. Ruddock the Robin has just given Alfred your message," said Grandad smiling gently.

"He has indeed Miss Bobbin," said Alfred politely.

Bobbin leapt into Grandad's arms, hugging him tightly. She then turned to Alfred and greeted him formally, "Good morning Alfred, I am so happy to see you are well. I think I saw you last night flying over my house quite late at night. Was it you?

"Possibly, possibly my dear Miss Bobbin, I visit you every night. How are you and your Mummy and Daddy?" asked Alfred.

"We are all well thank you Alfred. But I am most worried. I believe Queen Celandine has been calling to me. I'm worried something's not right with the fairies," said Bobbin, her voice now trembling slightly as a teardrop ran down her cheek.

Grandad gently wiped the tear away with his bright polka-dotted handkerchief.

Manu quickly sensed Bobbin's distress and ran round to her front, sat and looked up at her with love and concern in his eyes. Bobbin saw her dog's concern and knelt down and hugged him. Manu wagged his tail.

"Queen Celandine said she would call to you," said Alfred. "Your connection to her must be very strong" and flapped his wings showing how important this all was. "The problem is Miss Bobbin that the fairies are dangerously short of wood to burn for their fires to keep them warm in this freezing weather and unable to cook hot food of course" and flapped his wings again.

"Yes," confirmed Grandad, "Their wood pile can be low this time of year, especially after the Yule celebration, but usually they have a couple of weeks to bring in more wood. But this year the freeze has come early and they have been caught out" and paused thinking, "We must think about this problem and get moving the first thing in the morning."

Alfred spoke with quite an authority to his friends, "Grandad, Miss Bobbin, I suggest you both go into the kitchen where it's so much warmer and we can plan our rescue through the kitchen window."

"That's such a good idea Alfred, can we Grandad, I'm getting cold," said the shivering Bobbin.

Grandad laughed, "I was just about to suggest that to you two."

"I was just about to suggest that also Bobbin," whispered Manu.

Back in the kitchen Grandad opened the window over the sink as Alfred silently swooped onto the window frame, flapped his wings once and settled himself comfortably.

"Would you like a bowl of stew Alfred," asked Gigi.

"That would be most welcome Gigi, thank you very much," said Alfred, "It's getting colder out here and it will keep me going for the rest of the day."

"Should we make a list?" asked Bobbin, "There seems so much to do."

Gigi appeared from her cooking range and gave Alfred his bowl of stew saying, "That's an excellent idea my precious" and from a drawer in the dresser she produced a notebook and rummaged in another drawer and found a pencil and sat at the kitchen table and looked at Grandad. "Well, get on with it" and winked at Bobbin.

"Right!" said Grandad, "First things first, don't you agree Alfred?"

"I most certainly do Grandad," replied the owl.

"Well!" said Grandad and frowned at Bobbin, "What do you think my dear girl?"

Gigi rolled her eyes with impatience and said, "Tell them Bobbin."

Bobbin thought for a moment then said confidently "Firewood for warmth" and looked at Grandad.

Grandad frowned for a moment and said "I have plenty of wood in my old barn, we can use the cart to carry it to the fairy wood and dear old Juniper to pull it, he'll like that, it makes him feel so important" and looked at Gigi who was writing in her notepad.

Gigi finished writing and looked up at Bobbin.

"Hot food," said Bobbin, "Gigi's winter stew and, of course, rich Wild Wood cake" and looked over at Alfred who looked up from eating his stew and nodded his agreement at her.

"In a nutshell Bobbin," cried Grandad, "I'm so proud of you. Aren't you Gigi?"

"Yes I am Grandad," said Gigi, gazing at Bobbin.

Bobbin stood quietly, one hand on her chin thinking, a frown on her face.

"What is it Miss Bobbin?" said Alfred with an enquiring look.

Bobbin took a deep breath and said slowly, "There's another problem I can see" and looked out of the window and stood quietly for another moment, then turned back and spoke to them:

"Something tells me that it is too cold for Herb-Robert to patrol the Oak Wood without a warm fire and hot stew to fortify him and that could let into the Fairy Wood any naughty folk from the High Moor and beyond."

Alfred flapped his wings several times in excitement as Grandad said loudly, "Of course Bobbin, we haven't thought of that. Well done my girl."

Gigi looked up from her writing and looked at Bobbin with interest asking herself silently *where has she gained such wisdom at her young age?*

"Alfred," said Grandad, "You must fly to Lord Devon and ask him to arrange for the Fairy Wood to be guarded until we get Herb-Robert and the fairies back on their feet again."

"I will Grandad and get young Burnet to tell you what Lord Devon is going to do," said Alfred enthusiastically and flew off calling over his shoulder, "I'll see you tomorrow at the Fairy Wood."

"And Grandad, I feel Queen Celandine asks us to leave for the Oak Wood this afternoon with the firewood and food and be prepared to stay there overnight if necessary," said Bobbin looking at Gigi and wondering how that thought came into her head.

Grandad and Gigi looked at each other then both began nodding at each other.

"Grandad, our Bobbin is right you know," said Gigi and looked at Bobbin in wonder.

"By golly! Of course, she's right Gigi! I've got my old Bell Tent in the shed and the stove that'll keep us warm through the night," said Grandad to Gigi, then turned and looked at Bobbin wide-eyed.

"Right Grandad," said Gigi, "you go and hitch up the cart to Juniper and load it up with firewood and I'll make up bedrolls for you both" and smiled at Bobbin. "You'll both be as warm as toast tonight and what an adventure!"

....

There were others from beyond the High Moor who conspired, watched and waited. Then they saw an opportunity to rob and steal the last of the fairy's wood and food for themselves and, as they watched and waited, they smiled confidently at each other and licked their lips in anticipation.

The rogue tribe of mountain foxes and their sometime supporters, a ragged gang of big brown rats, began slowly creeping across the High Moor towards the Fairy Wood in the dark, having being told by an outcaste crow, that Herb-Robert was no longer patrolling the Oak Wood. These sly foxes and nasty rats came together to make their naughty plans in the darkness.

....

The Lord Devon was listening intently to what Alfred was saying to him, gently interrupting when he needed the owl to repeat what Bobbin had said. He then thanked his councillor, lifted his head and gazed up at the frozen treetops above him thinking. It was several moments in time before the Lord Devon made up his mind and spoke to Alfred.

"My dear friend and Councillor Alfred, please arrange for one of your messengers to visit Queen Celandine and assure her our help is on the way."

"I'll summon my nephew Burnet," said Alfred solicitously.

"Thank you Alfred," replied the Red Deer. "Also, another messenger to ask Talon the Crow and also Patience the High Moor Heron to watch out for any scallywags from the mountains beyond the High Moor, who may be thinking of taking advantage of the fairies' troubles."

Alfred flapped his wings and said, "I'll ask Hernshaw to send his friend Flash the Kingfisher to fly up there straight away Lord Devon. But who shall guard the Fairy Wood though?"

Lord Devon nodded at Alfred and lifted his head and said, "Yes Alfred, my thought is that I and Lady Titania with our son Oberon will camp in the Fairy Wood for the next few nights. Oberon and I will patrol the wood, and perhaps you would ask Bardon and Blade the Badger Brothers to help us."

"They would be delighted," cried Alfred happily, "They both enjoy nothing more than a good rough and tumble!"

"Excellent Alfred," said Lord Devon almost absent-mindedly and lifted his head in thought once more and said, "I'll ask my friend Reynard to go to Grandad's and tell him our plan, then to escort him to the Fairy Wood. I know my Lady Titania will be pleased to see Miss Bobbin."

Alfred looked at his lifelong friend and said admiringly, "I believe you have thought of everything..."

The Lord Devon quickly shook his antlers once saying, "It is we, you and I who have hopefully thought of everything my dear friend!" and lowered his head respectfully. "It is you Alfred who stimulate me in my thoughts. It is what good councillors do, subtly putting sensible thoughts in my head, then letting me believe they were my ideas."

....

Juniper the Donkey was hitched up to Grandad's cart which was loaded with firewood, Gigi's winter stew and fruit cake along with the Bell Tent, stove and enough food for supper that evening and breakfast in the morning. Plus, two large sacks of Hay for Juniper and another for their bedding that would keep them both warm throughout the freezing night to come.

"Manu," said Bobbin, "you can tuck up with me."

Manu waged his tail.

Juniper called through the kitchen door, "Reynard the silly fox is at the garden gate" and turned to Bobbin's dog, "You're not going to get under my feet are you Manu?"

Manu looked up at Juniper with one eyebrow raised "Only up your nose you silly donkey."

"We mustn't call Reynard a silly fox anymore Juniper," said Bobbin laughing.

"Grandad," called Juniper, "Manu just called me a silly donkey!" and laughed at Manu and stuck his tongue out.

"Behave yourselves you two and you Reynard," said Grandad smiling at Bobbin.

....

Moonbeam the Otter had been visiting his cousins who lived along the river and smaller brooks of the High Moor. The frozen brooks and the edges of the river were fun for the Otter who would leap off the side of a brook and skate across the ice to the other side. Then jump in the air, landing heavily on the ice and laughing in delight as the ice broke and he sank into the water and swam to the bottom searching for his favourite mussels and tasty crayfish hiding under the rocks.

Having eaten his breakfast, Moonbeam chased some ducks playfully enjoying his favourite pastime when he spotted Patience the High Moor Heron across the river speaking with Talon the Crow, who was perched on a low branch of his riverside cedar tree.

Moonbeam whistled to them both. Patience and Talon turned their heads and seeing Moonbeam flapped their wings once, indicating to the Otter they needed to speak to him.

The Otter dived into the water and with a flick of his powerful tail swam rapidly across the river to the far side. Once out of the water Moonbeam ran up to Patience and shook himself so vigorously that the spray from his coat splashed over the Heron and some even reached the Crow perched above.

Moonbeam then sat on his hind legs, raised his paws in greeting, unaware he had soaked the Heron and waited respectfully for him to finish his conversation with the Crow.

Patience smiled indulgently at the Otter and looked up at Talon who shook his head smiling at the Heron.

"Hello Moonbeam," said Patience, wiping water from his chest feathers with a wing, "I heard you have been visiting your cousins and had hoped I would see you."

Moonbeam waved his paws, "Yes I have Patience. Is there anything wrong?"

"Yes there is," replied the Heron and looked up at the old Crow, "Talon has just told me, that the mountain foxes and those rascals the Brown Rats are going to invade the Fairy Wood while Herb-Robert is laid up unwell. They wouldn't dare if Herb-Robert was fighting fit!"

"Wow!" cried Moonbeam, "I had better get back and help guard the Fairy Wood Patience."

Patience flapped his wings in excitement "Yes Moonbeam, get yourself back and report to the Lord Devon and tell him that as soon as I, or my friend Talon see any of those mountain rascals my friend here" and pointed at the Crow "will have a trusted messenger fly to the Fairy Wood and tell him"

....

Grandad and Bobbin arrived at the Fairy Wood later than planned, after stopping on the way to feed young rabbits and squirrels generous helpings of Gigi's hot winter stew and rich Wild Wood fruit cake. It was not before time, as the animals were all very hungry and cold. But after eating Gigi's stew and winter cake they felt much better as their mothers took them off to their beds where they would sleep and recover from the cold. Grandad said he would leave them what was left of the food when he and Bobbin returned from the Fairy Wood and told himself that Gigi would have to make more of her Winter Stew before this winter was over.

Juniper was humming a tune to himself as he pulled the cart through the Wild Wood. Reynard was leading the way, his nose stuck up in the air, his bushy tail straight out behind him. Manu and Bobbin were walking together and Grandad was beside Juniper his hand resting on the donkey's shoulder and, every now and then, gently patting him.

Reynard turned his head and said, "Don't you know another tune Juniper you silly donkey?"

"No, he doesn't," said Manu, and stuck his tongue out at Reynard. "I like your tune Juniper."

"Grandad," said Reynard, "Manu has stuck his tongue out to me."

Grandad winked at Bobbin and said "Now you two behave yourselves" and said to Juniper, "Do you know another tune by any chance, you have been humming that one all the way through the Wild Wood."

"Yes I do Grandad," said Juniper, "I've only been humming this one to annoy Reynard" and stuck his tongue out at the fox.

Reynard turned as Manu laughed. "Right Grandad, I'm going to tell my Lord Devon that Juniper and Manu have been naughty to me!"

"Be quiet," said Grandad gently, "all of you silly folk, stop this at once or I'll be speaking to the Lord Devon myself."

"Sorry Reynard, sorry Grandad," said Juniper smiling and winking at Manu.

"Sorry Reynard, sorry Grandad," said Manu smiling and winking at Juniper.

There was a pause as they waited for Reynard to apologise.

"Well Reynard?" said Grandad.

"Oh alright," said the exasperated fox "sorry Juniper, sorry Manu."

....

The light was fading on the High Moor. Thick cloud had formed in the late afternoon making it even darker.

The temperature had dropped even further and the frozen snow made a crunching sound beneath the feet of some two dozen creatures as they crept and slinked through the tufted grasses and stunted bushes.

They made no sound themselves, but unable to mask the sound of their feet, the rogue Foxes and nasty Brown Rats dropped their bellies to the ground and crawled and slithered through the frozen and frosted winter vegetation, as they began their skulking descent from the High Moor to the Fairy Wood.

....

Talon the Crow was perched waiting in the warmth of his cedar tree, comfortably surrounded by soft, slender branches of pine leaves that wrapped around him like a blanket denying any bitterly cold draft from reaching him, when a much younger crow weaving skilfully through the foliage landed on his branch, folded his wings and dropped his head respectfully and waited.

"I see you young Meadow Crow-Foot, what have you to tell me?" spoke Talon to his grandson.

Meadow lifted his head and held himself upright and addressed his father's father:

"Chief Talon, I have seen and heard the Foxes and Rats from beyond our Moor nearing the Fairy Wood. They will arrive there sometime sooner than later this evening" then dropped his head once more and waited.

"Thank you Meadow my boy, you have done well, very well indeed," said Talon in a much gentler tone, betraying his love for the young crow, "Come with me and speak with Patience the Heron. He waits by the river."

Patience listened carefully to Meadow Crow-Foot's tidings and smiled at Talon, complimenting him on his young crow's hearing and eyesight and asking, "Talon would you ask young Meadow to fly to the edge of the Fairy Wood, where Moonbeam the Otter and the two badger brothers are waiting and tell them?"

"Did you hear what Patience has said Meadow?" asked Talon.

"I have Chief Talon," answered the young crow flapping his wings in excitement.

"Then off you go, my dear boy and be careful," said Talon gently.

....

With Bobbin now leading the tired Juniper gently by his halter, Grandad, Manu and Reynard entered the Fairy Wood. There by the huge Yew tree, the Fairy Queen Celandine was waiting for them, with a tired-looking Herb-Robert holding his Fighting Pole standing next to her, the Queen's hand resting on her consort's free arm.

At her other side stood the majestic Lord Devon smiling down at Grandad, while Lady Titania and their son Oberon waited behind the Lord Devon smiling at Bobbin.

The Fairy Queen gave a dazzling smile at Bobbin, "Dear child you received my message" and stepped forward and took Bobbin's hands in hers. "We are so very relieved to see you so soon. It seems you and Grandad haven't wasted a moment in coming to our aid."

Alfred the Owl landed silently on the rail of Grandad's cart and smiled at Bobbin and turned to the Fairy Queen and waited.

"We came as quick as we could Celandine and will spend the night here helping your people to the firewood and distribute the food," said Bobbin looking at Grandad.

"Yes," agreed Grandad, addressing the Fairy Queen "let's get that done as quickly as we can. Then we can deal with those rascals from the mountains."

Queen Celandine turned to Herb-Robert and whispered in his ear, then turned back to Bobbin.

Herb-Robert ran to the other side of the Yew and gave a whistle and immediately all the other fairies appeared and waited by the Yew each carrying a large bowl to carry Gigi's food and a wheelbarrow to hold the firewood. "One at a time my dears," called Herb-Robert "go and collect your food and firewood from Grandad."

Bobbin held the Fairy Queen's warm hands. "It seems Bobbin that we never have time to just sit and talk. You must help Grandad and I must see to my people at this time."

"Perhaps Celandine, we will have more time in the spring and summer when I visit," said Bobbin, as the Fairy Queen kissed both her cheeks.

"Then I shall arrange for us to have a picnic on the first day of summer and we will dance into the night," answered the Fairy Queen. "I must go my dear to my people, I will see you before you and Grandad leave in the morning. Now go to Lady Titania and Oberon, they await you."

Bobbin, Titania and Oberon embraced each other eagerly, Titania and Oberon laying their heads on Bobbin's shoulders as she cuddled their necks. Oberon being especially careful as his antlers were now fully grown.

The Lord Devon smiled at the three friends and walked over to speak with Grandad, thanking Juniper and Reynard for their help first and then saying hello to Manu.

"Greetings Grandad, I hope you and Gigi are both well and thank you both for all your help to our friends of the Wild Wood and, of course, Queen Celandine and her folk," said the Red Deer.

"You and all our woodland folk are always on our minds Lord Devon and happy to help with anything," answered Grandad.

"Once again, thank you Grandad. Herb-Robert is sending his gardeners over to help with the distribution. Perhaps you could leave it to them and I'll also ask them to help you pitch your tent for the night," announced Lord Devon.

....

Meadow Crow-Foot saw Moonbeam with the badgers Bardon and Blade, the three of them brandishing wooden poles much like the one Herb-Robert was armed with. The badger brothers were pushing and striking each other playfully and laughing each time one of them managed to strike the other. Moonbeam was sat upright on his hind legs giggling delightfully at the antics of his friends when the young crow landed on a branch of a tree just above their heads and flapped his wings.

The otter and the brothers stopped their playing and looked at the crow who said "The mountain rascals are almost here. Moonbeam, Patience says you must tell Lord Devon immediately" and stopped, listened and said, "Can you hear that noise?"

The otter and the badgers cocked their ears and listened. "What is that sound Meadow?" asked Bardon.

"It's the sound of their feet on the frozen snow. You had better hurry Moonbeam," urged Meadow.

....

"Reynard!" said Lord Devon, steely-eyed and with anger in his voice, "my dear friend, you will stay here with Grandad, Miss Bobbin and my Lady Titania. Guard them with your life!" and looked at them with a smile. "Should any of those rogues get past us then you deal with them Reynard."

Lord Devon then turned to Herb-Robert: "You and your Fighting Pole stay with your Queen and deal with any intruder in your own way" and looked at Oberon, "Follow me my son."

"Oh dear," said Juniper, "We'll never get Reynard's nose out of the air now."

"Take care, my Lord," called Alfred as the two Red Deer sped off to the edge of the Fairy Wood followed by Moonbeam the Otter giggling with excitement.

....

Bardon and Blade raised their poles and braced themselves as a big, ragged Fox stepped out of the long grass, with a vicious-looking Brown Rat close behind him. Meadow Crow-Foot squawked loudly from a tree.

"Let me introduce myself to you badgers," said the Fox slyly. "My name is Grey Tooth, I am the leader of the Mountain Foxes and I want what you have" and gave a crooked smile. "And this is my friend Hobday, he is the chief of the Mountain Rats. He also wants what you have. So, I suggest you step to one side and let us get on with it." A dozen other Foxes and Brown Rats appeared from the long grass and stared menacingly at the two badgers.

Bardon and Blade both shouted back at the Foxes and Rats, "Try and make us!" and brandished their weapons as they became aware they had been joined by others. "Hello Bardon, hello Blade. We thought we might be of some help," said Larkspur the Weasel and Mouse Ear the Stoat together. "Although now we are wondering if it was such a good idea" as they stared at the Foxes and Rats fearfully.

The badgers laughed in delight. "You are both very welcome! Here take our cudgels" and handed them their smaller sticks.

"Well, I did warn you!" shouted the Grey Tooth and ran towards them with all his villainous companions close behind shouting dreadful threats.

The four brave defenders of the Fairy Wood raised their weapons and prepared to stand their ground, as they heard the thunder of Lord Devon's and Oberon's hooves as they pounded through the edge of the wood. Then, leaping over their friends' heads, landed among the Mountain Foxes and Rats. Lord Devon and Oberon then dropped their heads to the ground and violently shook their antlers and charged, scattering the mountain scallywags, as the badger brothers with Larkspur and Mouse Ear thrashed about them with their sticks.

Grey Tooth the Fox was the first to take fright, turn and run, quickly followed by Hobday the Rat, with all the other mountain scallywags falling and stumbling over each other to escape as Moonbeam the Otter snapping at their heals chased them up to the High Moor. There Talon the Crow and his tribe waited for them with a warning never to return to the High Moor or the Fairy Wood again.

"I enjoyed that father," said Oberon breathlessly as he and Lord Devon walked back into the Fairy Wood, with their comrades who were loudly congratulating themselves and telling each other how brave they had been.

The Lord Devon looked at his son with fondness and laid his head across Oberon's shoulder and said quietly, "I am proud of you my son, but remember we only use our fearsome strength and antlers against the enemies of the folk we are duty bound to protect. And yes, I enjoyed that too" and smiled lovingly at Oberon. "Ah look! They have made a fire to welcome us back."

"Ah here you all are," cried Queen Celandine. "Albert told us of all your brave deeds. He says we won't be disturbed by those mountain scallywags again. Come and sit by the fire" and called on her fairy folk to bring some of Gigi's stew and handfuls of Grandad's sweet hay for Lord Devon and Oberon.

Bobbin and Titania walked over to Lord Devon and his son, Titania gently laying her head over her Lord's shoulder as Bobbin threw her arms round Oberon's neck and kissed his forehead. The badger brothers, Larkspur and Mouse Ear with Moonbeam sat round the fire and ate hot bowls of stew and fruit of the forest tea made by the fairies.

Reynard the Fox walked formally up to Lord Devon, stood quietly with his nose still in the air and waited to be seen.

Oberon saw his friend first and whispered to Reynard "Your nose is in the air you silly fox" and giggled.

"No, it's not Oberon and when your father sees me I shall tell him you called me a silly fox" and poked his tongue out at Oberon and giggled to himself as the Lord Devon turned his head and saw the fox and his tongue.

"Tell me Reynard why is your tongue out and pointed at my son?" keeping his face serious and pretending to be angry.

Shocked he had been caught by the Lord Devon, the fox dropped his head to the ground and waited to be told off.

An expectant silence came to those seated round the fire, as they all waited and wondered to see what was going to happen next when Oberon stood and walked over to Reynard and stood by his side and addressed his father.

"Father," said Oberon looking down on his friend the fox and then up at the Lord Devon, "it is not what you think. Reynard told me how thirsty he is and I said show me your tongue" and looked over at Bobbin for help.

Bobbin quickly walked over to Oberon and Reynard and waited respectfully for Lord Devon to address her.

The Lord Devon still struggling to keep a straight face said, "Miss Bobbin, perhaps you have something to add?" and glanced over at Grandad and flashed just a trace of a knowing smile at him. Grandad returned a broad grin and both looked away from each other in case others should see.

Bobbin looked Lord Devon in the eye as Titania sedately walked to Bobbin's side and stood quietly gazing at her Lord.

"Lord Devon," said Bobbin formally, carefully choosing her words "I have seen the playful exchanges between Oberon and Reynard several times and, although silly to others, Grandad and I are amused by them. But my Grandad tells me there is a time and a place for all things" and looked down at the fox and stroked his head. "What I can tell you" and looked Lord Devon confidently in his eyes once more, "Reynard never once left our side while you and the others were away dealing with those mountain rascals."

"Well said Miss Bobbin," called Alfred the Owl from a branch just above Lord Devon's head, "Well said indeed!"

"We agree!" said the badger brothers Bardon and Blade.

Moonbeam the Otter giggled and clapped his paws together as Larkspur and Mouse Ear sat cuddling each other with puzzled looks on their faces not knowing what to say.

Lord Devon shook his antlers once and silence fell round the fire. "My friend Reynard, please lift your head and look at me."

The Fox lifted his head and looked into the Red Deer's eyes and swallowed back his fear.

"It seems I am mistaken Reynard and ask for your forgiveness," said Lord Devon and looked over at Grandad with a twinkle in his eyes.

"There is nothing to forgive my Lord, I was being silly again" answered Reynard honestly.

"Well said Reynard," shouted Alfred.

"Good for you," called the badger brothers with Moonbeam sat next to them giggling, and from the background Juniper's voice was heard saying, "Oh dear look, Reynard's nose is in the air again."

Everyone laughed apart from Reynard of course as Grandad looked at his pocket watch and said to Bobbin "It's time for bed."

"Night night don't let the Lady Birds bite," called the animals and birds, as Bobbin cuddled Titania and Oberon and stroked Reynard's head and followed Grandad to the tent with Manu at her heels.

....

The first flurries of snow had begun to find their way into the Fairy wood, driven by a bitterly cold wind that had gathered strength as it swept across the High Moor. The temperature of the early evening suddenly dropped and Jack Frost again walked across the land and tightened his grip on the already frozen wood.

"Good lord it's getting very cold Bobbin," said Grandad as they and Manu made their way back to the tent. "Let's hope the Fairy Gardeners remembered to light our stove."

"So do I Grandad," responded Bobbin, who was now really starting to feel the freezing cold. "But where is Juniper Grandad?"

"There he is" and Grandad pointed to the cart which was now covered with a canvas rainproof sheet over a mound of dry leaves that the Fairies had stored in the autumn, and under the leaves was Juniper snug and warm. "Are you warm enough Juniper?" called Grandad.

"Yes I am, thank you Grandad, I am all cosy and warm. Please don't wake me too early in the morning," answered the donkey all dreamy-eyed and slurred-voiced.

"Do you want a blanket over you Juniper?" asked Bobbin, "It's beginning to snow!"

"Yes please Miss Bobbin," said the tired donkey being polite, "I probably won't need it though."

Grandad looked up at the chimney sticking out of the top of the tent, "Ah, the Fairies did light our stove. We'll be warm as toast tonight."

Bobbin looked up and saw smoke rising out of the chimney and being immediately snatched away by the freezing wind, scattering and quickly disappearing among the oaks and bushes.

Grandad pulled aside the tent door and stepped aside to let Bobbin in and said to Manu "Give yourself a shake before you come in my little friend."

Manu gave a single "Woof", shook himself, entered the tent and laid down by the warm stove and asked Grandad, "Anything to eat before I go to sleep?"

"Good idea Manu," said Grandad and turned to Bobbin. "We'll heat up a small bowl of Gigi's stew for tonight and have a nice big breakfast in the morning before we leave. Would you like that Bobbin? It'll warm you up before going to bed."

"Yes please, I am a bit hungry. Manu when you have warmed up come and snuggle up with me. We can keep each other warm tonight," said Bobbin.

....

There was a carpeting of snow in the Fairy Wood that was not too deep, answering the woodlander's prayer to Brigid, for any snowfall to be not too deep. The wind had blown itself out and the Oak Wood was at peace with itself once more.

Grandad gently shook Bobbin awake and asked "Did you sleep well my child?" and saw Manu open one eye then the other and said, "Good morning Grandad, I had a lovely sleep."

"Up you get then Manu and go and see if Juniper's awake yet," said Grandad as Bobbin turned over and said "Good morning Grandad" and smiled.

"Up you get Bobbin, let's have a nice breakfast then go home to Gigi," said Grandad smiling.

First Day of Summer

Bobbin was sat at the kitchen table eating an early evening meal with Mummy. Daddy had just arrived home after a long day at the cottage hospital. He had quickly kissed her and Mummy saying "Give me five minutes to change and wash my hands. And!" and raised a finger, "Do you know I'm on holiday for a week? Hurrah!" and ran upstairs chuckling to himself, so pleased to be home.

Mummy's face lit up and smiled across the table at Bobbin, "Now you know you're spending a few days at Grandad's while Daddy and I have some time on our own?" she said taking Bobbin's hands in hers. "You don't mind do you Bobs?"

"Oh no Mummy," replied Bobbin choosing her words with care, being careful not to show how pleased she really was, "I'll be busy helping Grandad and Gigi and seeing all my friends that live in the Wild Wood. Can I take Manu please?"

Manu heard his name mentioned and pricked up his floppy ears on hearing Bobbin was going to Grandad's and nudged her and wagged his tail.

"Yes of course, Daddy asked Grandad yesterday and he and Gigi are looking forward to seeing you," said Mummy. "Here comes Daddy" and went to the fridge and took out a bowl of his favourite salad.

"Do you know," said Daddy sitting himself down at the table, "I could have sworn I've just seen a big bird perched on Bobbin's bedroom window sill. I turned the light on but there was nothing there," he said frowning. "Perhaps it was just a shadow though" and shrugged, picked up his fork and reached for the salad cream.

Bobbin felt Manu stir. She looked down and saw he was looking up at her wagging his tail. Quickly without her parents being aware, she rolled her eyes towards the stairs, signalling Manu to go and see if it was Alfred waiting for her.

Manu gave a low "Woof" and ran silently up the stairs as Bobbin said to Daddy "I'm looking forward to seeing Grandad and Gigi."

"Yes," said daddy smiling, "you really seem to enjoy yourself there, don't you" and looked at Mummy. "It gives us a chance for a few days away together by ourselves, although we do miss you Bobbin" and popped a small plum tomato into his mouth. "We'll drop you off the day after tomorrow and pick you up at the weekend."

"I was telling Mummy how much I enjoy going to Grandad's and seeing all my Wild Wood friends, Daddy," said Bobbin, hearing Manu running down the stairs.

Manu sat next to Bobbin and looked up at her saying in his quiet voice, "It's Albert, he says not to hurry, finish your supper he has plenty of time this evening."

"Do you know," said Mummy frowning, "I would swear Manu was speaking to you then."

Bobbin laughed to hide her surprise. "He was, he was speaking doggy talk to me" and looked down at Manu and ruffled the silky hair on the top of his head playfully, "and I understood every word," she said honestly.

Once in her bedroom, Bobbin went to the window, opened it and said eagerly, "Alfred, I'm so sorry to keep you waiting. I'm so pleased to see you."

It was just beginning to grow dark after a lovely warm, late spring day, two days before the First Day of Summer and the fairy's picnic.

All the birds and animals of the Wild Wood were invited to this celebration of a time of plenty, where throughout the summer food and fuel would be gathered and stored ready for the coming winter. Those who had experienced hunger and cold in the Deep Mid-Winter days of January and February would solemnly remind each other to gather and prepare and not be caught out by early frosts and freezes.

"And I Miss Bobbin, am so very pleased to see you this evening," said Alfred warmly, "You are in for a wonderful time at the picnic, especially as it's so much warmer and brighter than Yuletide."

"If it doesn't rain of course," spoke Manu cynically.

Alfred looked down his beak at Manu and replied "It never rains at Litha" and flapped his wings twice.

It was the fairies who called this time of year Litha, the ancient name for the Summer Solstice. Queen Celandine would dress brightly in her summer silks. Her shoulders and head would be decorated with St John's Wort, known to the fairies as the Herb of the Sun and woven with flowers of both the Oak Wood and the surrounding meadows. There she would lead her folk who had gathered by her Yew Tree out of the wood and into the meadow, escorted by her beloved Herb-Robert who would dress in his Forest Green trousers and felt boots that reached to his knees. His coat of a darker Forest Green would be buttoned up to his neck and the By-cocked hat he would wear decorated with a Sparrow Hawk's wing feather, jauntily pinned by a White Crystal broach and, as always, in the belt of his jacket would be a cudgel and in his right hand his Fighting Staff.

The fairy gardeners would then run from the Oak Wood onto the meadow on Herb-Robert's signal, pushing their wheelbarrows laden with delicious salads to be eaten at the picnic. To be followed by Pixie Pears, Honey Cakes and Mallow Fruit.

Queen Celandine would then step from the wood to be followed by an excited and eager crowd of fairy children and their parents singing and dancing.

"Now Miss Bobbin," said Alfred seriously, "we haven't seen you for weeks it seems, but we all know you have been at school and unable to visit us," he said gently. "Queen Celandine is so much looking forward to seeing you at her picnic, everyone's so excited at seeing you again" and looked down at Manu and said sarcastically "Bring Manu, if you want."

Manu gave another of his low "Woofs" and looked up at Bobbin and grinned.

"Oh, and Miss Bobbin," Alfred continued, "When you get the chance would you have a quiet word with Moonbeam, he's been chasing the ducks again, in spite of Hernshaw's disapproval. He really shouldn't do that, this time of year."

"Why?" asked the curious Bobbin.

Alfred thought for a moment on how he would explain the mating season, and then replied carefully, "This is the time of year the ducks are nesting and about to lay their eggs. In a few weeks they will welcome their ducklings into the world Miss Bobbin. New life, new life!" he said seriously. "Hernshaw has asked me to do something about that silly otter and I thought of you."

....

On arrival at Grandad's cottage, Bobbin kissed her Daddy quickly and let Manu out of the car first then followed swinging her rucksack over a shoulder, opened the garden gate and walked up the pathway towards the front door. Followed by an excited Manu. There they stopped and looked into the apple orchard and saw Grandad's dog Bonnie wandering round the orchard wagging her tail.

Manu "Woofed" a greeting and wagged his tail.

Bobbin called, "Hello Bonnie, what are you doing in the orchard on your own? Does Gigi know you're out here?"

"Oh yes Bobbin, hello Manu," replied Bonnie, "Gigi let me out of the kitchen saying it was such a lovely warm day and good for my old bones."

Juniper appeared from behind the apple trees. "Hello Miss Bobbin, Grandad's in his shed" and looked at Manu. "Do try not to get under my feet" and took a large mouthful of fresh green grass.

"Do try not to get up my nose," replied Manu and poked out his tongue at the donkey.

"Now stop bickering you two!" said Bobbin trying not to laugh, "Or I'll tell Grandad."

Juniper ignored Manu's remark and said to Bobbin sweetly, "Grandad always lets me eat this tasty spring grass, it's full of wildflowers which gives it such a lovely flavour."

Bobbin heard Grandad call, "Is that you Bobbin? I'm in the shed."

"I'm coming Grandad," said Bobbin and patted Juniper's shoulder and walked round the side of the cottage. Manu and Juniper laughed at each other.

"There you are my lovely girl," said Gigi standing at the kitchen door, "Give me a hug."

Grandad came out of the shed and kissed Bobbin's cheek and said, "Shall we go to the Secret Lake this afternoon and speak to Moonbeam? Albert told you he was being naughty didn't he?"

"Yes he did Grandad," replied Bobbin. "And the sooner we speak to him, the better for the ducks I think" she added wisely.

"Yes it certainly will be," smiled Grandad. "I've arranged with Alfred to meet Hernshaw there as well."

In the kitchen, Gigi gave Grandad his bag and said to Bobbin, "There's sandwiches and sweet tea for you both when you get to the lake. Don't be too long Grandad, we've a long day tomorrow at the fairy picnic. Oh, and give me your rucksack Bobbin and I'll hang up your summer dress. Did you see Bonnie?"

"I did Gigi. She seems happy enough," smiled Bobbin.

"Oh" said Gigi "she's at her happiest wandering and sniffing round the orchard and chatting with Juniper."

....

The rushes and reeds were now fully grown on the shore line of the Secret Lake. On the water, here and there was a gathering of Water Lilies in flower, with Damson and Dragon Flies hovering over them, then leaping and dancing from one Lily to another, and the first of the ducklings dutifully in line following their mothers, looking like a line of soldiers.

The Water Boatmen were rowing themselves out of the way of the ducks, their boat-shaped bodies and oar-like back legs lighter than the water and breathing from bubbles stored round their bodies and under their wings.

At the lakeside, a myriad of wildflowers, reeds and rushes were giving a bright blush of colour. For the Water Violets and Water Soldiers were in full bloom. The Water Forget-me-Nots, Marsh Marigolds and the Yellow Flag Iris, each a crowning glory of the Secret Lake in the summertime.

Grandad and Bobbin were expected and all their old friends had gathered at the top of the lake. Hernshaw the Heron was waiting, with Moonbeam and Flash the Kingfisher. Moonbeam was smiling nervously to himself, as Hernshaw had told him he was going to be Told Off for chasing the ducks. Flash was pleased as Moonbeam was still taking his fish.

There was Alfred the Owl, who was perched on the alter in the Secret Grove, just a short distance away who would quietly cast his judicious eyes over the proceedings and report to the Lord Devon himself. Who always showed interest in naughty behaviour by any of the Wild Wood folk.

Grandad and Bobbin arrived early in the afternoon and Bobbin gasped at the beauty of the Secret Lake in all its late spring glory. "Oh Grandad," she said, "it was covered with ice the last time we were here" and took his hand, "It's so beautiful."

Grandad stopped and looked at the lake for a moment and then turning to face his Great Granddaughter, "Yes it is Bobbin and all this must be protected."

Bobbin looked up at her Great Grandfather frowning, "Protected Grandad? What do you mean?"

Grandad smiled down at her saying quietly, "When you're a little bit older my lovely girl, we'll have a chat about that" and walked on and pointed to the top of the lake, "There they are, all waiting for us."

....

Bobbin looked down at the Otter and smiled at him gently, her expression showing the high regard she felt for him.

Moonbeam had been nervous when told he was going to be Told Off, especially when it was going to be Miss Bobbin herself, as he loved and respected her so much in his silly Otter way.

"My dear Moonbeam," said Bobbin quietly, "let us go over there" and pointed "and I'll sit on that log and you sit next to me."

Moonbeam giggled nervously and ran over to the log and sat on his hind legs and held his paws up respectfully. Bobbin followed and sat opposite facing the Otter.

Alfred nodded his agreement and now waited with interest how Bobbin would commence her Telling Off of Moonbeam, knowing he would be giving a full report of this to the Lord Devon and Queen Celandine.

Hernshaw the Heron looked at his friend Moonbeam and felt sorry for him but knew he must be Told Off to maintain the peace and tranquillity of the Wild Wood and the High Moor.

The two Badger brothers Bardon and Blade looked at each other both feeling sympathy for the Otter and agreed to comfort their friend Moonbeam by taking him back to Bardon's set and feeding him with a large bowl of their Woodland Spring Stew.

While Flash the Kingfisher flew off, suddenly not wanting to witness Moonbeam's shame. For although he would grumble to Hernshaw about his fish being taken, he was always amused by the Otter's sometime naughtiness and antics.

Bobbin took Moonbeam's two front paws in her hands and held them tenderly and looked with her big soft eyes into his. Moonbeam's eyes welled up with tears as he dropped his head, his two big dark eyes gazing up into hers. She let go of one of Moonbeam's paws and gently stroked the top of his head.

"Now Moonbeam," she said softly, and all the animals watching and listening leaned forward to hear the words that Bobbin spoke, "your good friend Hernshaw has spoken to you about chasing the ducks this time of year. He is so worried about your behaviour that he asked Alfred to help and so Alfred asked me to speak with you."

The woodland folk watching all looked at each other, nodded sagely and looked back at Moonbeam, who had dropped his head lower.

"But Moonbeam, I know you were just playing with the ducks and not being really naughty," said Bobbin.

Moonbeam lifted his head and nodded eagerly at Bobbin and his paw Bobbin had been holding the otter placed over her hand that held his other paw and all those watching and listening nodded their agreement at each other, as Alfred flapped his wings.

"But this time of year, when the ducks are nesting and getting ready to lay their eggs, it is most important you don't chase them. They must be left in peace to have their ducklings and bring them up safely," continued Bobbin, still with her soft gentle tones. A tear ran down Moonbeam's cheek as he said "Yes Miss Bobbin."

Bobbin quickly brushed the tear away and leaned forward and gave moonbeam a gentle hug saying, "And so dear Moonbeam, let there be no more of chasing ducks this summer and I'll tell Lord Devon" and glanced over at Alfred "you didn't need a Telling Off, just having this explained to you. You won't do this anymore will you Moonbeam?"

Moonbeam looked at Bobbin wide-eyed answering "Oh no Miss Bobbin, I won't. I'll never chase the ducks again," he said excitedly.

Grandad, who had been standing with Manu in the background, clapped and Manu gave a loud "Woof" and wagged his tail. Alfred flapped his wings again with Hernshaw, while the badger brothers began wrestling each other in happiness. Moonbeam ran to Hernshaw and ran tight circles round him in happiness.

Bobbin stood and walked over to Alfred. "Did I do the right thing," she asked feeling slightly uncertain.

Alfred flapped his wings for the third time and said quietly to her, "Miss Bobbin, you have a wisdom beyond your years child."

"Come Bobbin," spoke Grandad, "Let's get back to the cottage, Gigi is cooking us a roast this evening" and whispered, "I'm very proud of you" as Manu stood gazing up at his beloved Bobbin, his tall wagging.

Bobbin waved her goodbye to Alfred and the others and called "I'll see you all tomorrow!"

"Bye Miss Bobbin, we'll see you tomorrow," they all replied together and Moonbeam whistled and waved at her.

....

After Gigi had tucked her up in bed, kissed her forehead and wished her a peaceful sleep, Bobbin slept until well after dawn. In fact, it was Ruddock the Robin who tapped lightly on her bedroom window and woke Manu, who was allowed to sleep at the bottom of her bed while at Grandad's and Gigi's cottage.

"Wake up you two," the Robin called, "It's the Fairy picnic today and young Oberon and that silly fox Reynard will be arriving soon to escort you there. We're all waiting!" and flitted off back into the Wild Wood.

"Did you hear that Bobbin?" said Manu sleepily.

Bobbin, who still had both her eyes closed, said wearily, "I did. I suppose we had better get up" and opened her eyes, peeled off the duvet and put her feet on the carpet. "Come on Manu, rise and shine."

....

Oberon and Reynard were nearing Grandad's cottage when Oberon stopped and turned to his friend the fox and asked with an expression of innocence "Reynard, do you remember at Yule when we escorted them" and gestured with his chin at the cottage "to the Fairy Wood and we got here early and you woke up most of the Wild Wood by shouting?" and avoided meeting the fox's eyes in case he laughed.

Reynard, whose nose was already in the air, stopped, frowned, dropped his nose and looked at Oberon in puzzlement. "What on earth are you talking about, you silly Red Deer?"

Oberon turned his face away from his friend and gritted his back teeth desperately trying to stifle a giggle. "You shouted, Grandad's still in bed," he just managed to say and gritted his teeth even tighter.

"No, I most certainly did not!" said the outraged Reynard in a loud angry voice.

Immediately, there followed an explosion of noise from the trees surrounding the cottage as the crows, rooks and pigeons took flight from their roosts protesting loudly, as both Manu in Bobbin's bedroom and Bonnie, who slept in the kitchen downstairs, barked several times.

Bobbin's door opened and Grandad appeared laughing, "We can all guess who startled our friends out there."

"There!" said Oberon grinning with delight, "You have done it again! Don't you ever learn?" as the sound of the chickens clucking loudly in the hen house came to their ears.

"Oh my!" exclaimed Reynard and dropped his head in shame.

"Not from where I am sitting young Oberon," said Burnet the Little Owl, "I think Alfred has to know about your leg pulling of poor Reynard."

Oberon and Reynard looked up in surprise and saw Burnet perched on a low branch of an old oak tree, almost invisible as he sat still and silent. The seasoned branches and twigs were the same colour and shades as his feathers.

"Ah!" cried Reynard, "That's got you Oberon" in a loud and excited voice causing another disturbance and protest among other birds that lived nearby.

....

"Come on you two, it's about time we got going," said Grandad, "We want to be there and watch the Fairies parade out of the Oak Wood and into the meadow," he said enthusiastically, "It's such a sight!"

In the garden, Gigi mounted Juniper and made herself comfortable. Grandad took the halters and guided Juniper up the garden, past his shed towards the gate that led into the Wild Wood.

Bobbin and Manu followed, both looking forward to seeing the fairies parade into the meadow. Bobbin was wearing her summer frock with a wreath of St John's Wort round her head, with Manu gently brushing up against her right leg and walking beside her.

As they reached the garden gate, Grandad opened it and they all passed through into the Wild Wood to be met by Oberon and Reynard, who both formally greeted them in the names of Queen Celandine of the Fairies and, of course, the ruler of the Wild Wood and the High Moor, the Lord Devon.

Bobbin ran forward and threw her arms round Oberon's neck and kissed his cheek saying "Your antlers are so big now Oberon."

"So is his head Miss Bobbin," said Reynard and laughed at the blushing Oberon.

Bobbin stepped over to the fox and knelt down beside him and stroked his head and shoulders lovingly. "Now Reynard," she said, "I know you are just both teasing each other, but there are others that would think you are being naughty. And we don't want that again. Do we?"

"Yes Miss Bobbin," said Burnet, who had silently flown down from his branch and was now perched on Grandad's garden gate. "It was Oberon pulling his leg again. Reynard falls for it every time" and flapped his wings like Alfred.

Gigi called back looking over her shoulder, "Now we've got all that nonsense behind us, let's get on."

With Gigi sat comfortably on Juniper, Bobbin and Manu followed into the Wild Wood.

Oberon lowered his antlers and greeted them formally while Reynard sat and raised his nose in the air.

Gigi greeted them, first asking Oberon how his parents were and remarking on the size of his antlers. She then turned to Reynard who now stood showing his respect. "My dear Reynard, the brush on your tail is truly eye-catching."

Oberon shook his antlers in delight while Reynard looked at the Red Deer and said in a whisper "Did you hear that Oberon, you silly Red Deer? I am eye-catching!"

Both Juniper and Manu laughed.

"I heard that!" called Grandad "Now let's all behave ourselves, shall we."

"I have been keeping an eye on them both," said Burnet from above their heads, "They have both been silly on the way here Grandad" and flew to a bush where they could all see him. "Hello Grandad, Gigi" and looked at Bobbin shyly, "Hello Miss Bobbin."

Bobbin smiled back at Burnet and saw a gathering of small animals waiting for them further down the path.

There were families of Rabbits, young and old with their clan leader Boss thumping his back foot on the ground with the others jumping and leaping in time to his thumps.

On the low-lying bushes, branches and twigs fallen from the trees above, Wood Mice, Field Mice, Dormice and Shrews lined up all calling at the tops of the tiny voices, "Hello Grandad, hello Gigi, hello Miss Bobbin, it's Litha! Have a happy day, don't eat too much."

In the trees and air above them, all the small garden birds of the Wild Wood flitted from one branch to another, each singing their different songs with Ruddock the Robin flying close to Bobbin calling, "Happy Litha, Miss Bobbin."

"What a racket," said Manu.

"No, it's not," said Bobbin, "It's joyous!" and skipped along the path with Manu running behind her.

Grandad called "Bobbin, look behind us."

Bobbin stopped and turned round and there walking slowly followed a herd of the small and gentle Fallow Deer. An old stag lead the way, with the does and fawns kept in a bunch for their safety by the young yearling stags. The herd would arrive in the Wild Wood every spring, after seeking permission from their much bigger cousin the Lord Devon.

"Should I greet them Grandad?" asked Bobbin.

Grandad looked at the old stag and raised his hand in greeting, "Yes Bobbin, wait here for him to reach you" and looked at Manu and pointed to him, "You come with me."

Manu looked at Bobbin questioningly.

"Yes Manu, you stay with Grandad," she said, "Just while I greet them."

Manu gave a low "Woof" and stayed with Grandad.

Grandad, who had stepped back behind Bobbin, said quietly, "His name is Whitethorn" and looked at the old Fallow Deer and added, "He is very wise and a good friend of Lord Devon."

Bobbin waited for the old stag to reach her, noting he was much smaller than the Red Deer, his antlers although fully grown were nothing compared with Lord Devon's or his son Oberon's. But, like Lord Devon, he had a composed and assured presence that left no doubt about who he was.

As the old stag reached her, he stopped and turned his head slightly, his eyes on Bobbin for the first time. He then raised his head high and shook his antlers in greeting at the smiling Bobbin and said, "Hello Miss Bobbin, I greet you on behave of my family and myself" and slowly lowered his antlers as the herd called together, "Hello Miss Bobbin, we're very pleased to meet you."

Bobbin spoke quietly, her voice measured, her words chosen. "Hello Whitethorn, and I am very pleased to meet you and I look forward to speaking with you later at the picnic" and looking over at his family she added, "And getting to know you all and if there's anything I can do for you."

The Fallow Deer raised his head again and shook his antlers once more, "And I look forward to our conversation Miss Bobbin, but I would not interrupt your picnic," he replied and lowered his head again.

Bobbin smiled and said gently "Speaking to you Whitethorn will not in any way interrupt my picnic."

"Then I will look forward to that Miss Bobbin" replied the stag.

Grandad called "Come on you two, we must get on."

....

Further down the Wild Wood path waited the weasels and stoats with their kittens and when they saw Grandad's party they formed family circles holding each other's paws and began to dance round in their circles, the kittens holding tightly to their parent's paws with everyone calling "Happy Litha, Miss Bobbin."

Juniper stopped and said sarcastically, "I expect they'll get under my feet Grandad."

"Let's hope so," said Manu laughing.

"Behave yourselves you two," called Reynard with his nose still in the air.

Bobbin skipped up to the weasels and stoats and clapped in time to their dancing.

"You behave yourself Reynard, you silly fox," said Juniper making Manu laugh even louder.

It was Oberon who called a stop to this nonsense. "Stop this silliness all of you now," he said, lowering his antlers and shaking them angrily, "It's Litha, so let us enjoy it" and turned to Reynard and said "Come on let's show an example to that silly donkey" and stepped on in a regal air just as his father the Lord Devon would, with Reynard the Fox, his nose in the air and his brush tail held high.

Juniper surprised at Oberon's remarks said to Manu, "Who does he think he is?"

Manu was about to answer when Bobbin said "Manu, please come and walk with me."

Gigi stroked Juniper's neck and said quietly, "You wasn't being naughty was you my lovely donkey?"

Juniper stopped in his tracks and said, "Oh no Gigi" and thought for a moment then said "Was I Gigi? I am sorry. Please don't tell Grandad."

Gigi answered winking at Grandad, "I won't tell him this time, will I Grandad."

"No don't tell me this time Gigi," answered Grandad.

"Thank you Gigi," said the relieved Juniper.

....

Hernshaw and his cousin Patience were waiting for them at the Secret Lake with Flash the Kingfisher perched on a Bull Rush next to them. Flash had been complaining again that Moonbeam was still taking his fish and both Hernshaw and Patience had tried to explain to him that is what Otters do, they eat fish. But Flash had not grasped that thought and continued with his complaining.

So now both the Herons were talking among themselves and ignoring Flash, who could not understand why, much to the amusement of Alfred and his young nephew Burnet, who had just arrived from Grandad's garden gate.

Bardon and Blade were sat eating wild apples watching as the smaller birds of the Wild Wood began gathering round them. Moonbeam was splashing about in the middle of the lake making a nuisance of himself among the Damson and Dragon Flies but staying well away from the ducks. While Mouse Ear and Larkspur hid behind an oak, waiting nervously to ask Alfred if they could go to the picnic and speak to Lord Devon.

On arrival at the Secret Lake, Grandad, Gigi and Bobbin greeted all their friends, with Bobbin quietly asking Hernshaw if Moonbeam was now behaving himself and leaving the ducks alone, while Gigi walked over to the badger brothers and spoke with them.

Alfred appeared among them all and said, "It's about time we made our way to the Fairy Meadow if we are to see the fairies' arrival, it's an amazing sight Miss Bobbin" flapped his wings once and called to Whitethorn the Fallow Deer a greeting saying, "Let's speak with Miss Bobbin this afternoon."

Whitethorn raised his antlers to Alfred and shook them twice.

The Fairy Meadow was covered with a shimmering carpet of wildflowers and grasses. A trembling, flowing sea of colour, gently waving in the warm summer breeze. Wild grasses of Crested Dogstail, Yellow Rattle and Fox and Cubs with summer flowers of Common Sorrel, Cow Slip, Lady's Bedstraw and Meadow Buttercups and Daisies, with Wild Carrot and Birds Feet Trefoil blessed the meadow.

In the centre of the meadow, a large circle and path that led to the Fairy Wood had been scythed that morning by the fairy gardeners, leaving the grass short and comfortable to sit on. At the far edge of the circle, there a solitary oak would give its shadow to this area in the heat of the afternoon. "A gift," said Alfred, "from Cernunnos, the Green Man whose spirit form will be watching closely from the Fairy Wood."

"There," pointed Grandad, "is Lord Devon and Lady Titania, let's go over there to them" and turned to Bobbin, "We walk round the circle, only the fairies are in the circle. Did you hear that Manu?" he said gently.

Manu looked up at Bobbin and said "Woof" and rolled his eyes impatiently.

Lord Devon and Lady Titania were stood at the side of the oak and both raised their heads in greeting. Lady Titania stepped forward as Bobbin walked eagerly towards her.

"Oh Titania, I am so pleased to see you. How are you? You look so well," said the breathless Bobbin, looking at her closely and put her arms round Titania's neck and hugged her.

"I am, I am my dear Bobbin and I have wonderful news," the Red Hind said quietly, "I am with child, I have new life in my tummy. I am so happy" she blushed and looked over at Lord Devon, "My Lord is so very pleased."

"Wow!" said Bobbin surprised and perplexed telling herself she would have to speak to Gigi on this subject.

"Yes indeed Bobbin, wow! Now there are only three of us but come late summer there will be four! How wonderful." Titania beamed with pleasure and looked at Lord Devon adoringly.

The Lord Devon looked at his Lady and said "You mustn't get excited, my dear Titania" and smiled at Bobbin.

Bobbin stepped closer to Lord Devon and greeted him formally, "Lord Devon, I am so very happy to see you once more and my congratulations on your wonderful news."

The huge Red Deer gazed into her eyes, "And I am very happy to see you again Miss Bobbin and looking forward to seeing you more often, one of these days" and left those last few words hanging in the air, as he caught sight of Reynard the Fox and said in a whisper, "The silly fox, the gods bless him" and smiled at Bobbin, "will make a fine guardian to my coming child.

I haven't told him yet, but when I do you will know because his nose will be even higher in the air than it is now" and laughed at his own joke.

"Can I tell Grandad and Gigi Lord Devon?" Bobbin asked wondering what he meant by 'one of these days'.

"My Lady Titania will tell them this afternoon. She wanted to tell you first" he smiled and turned his head towards the Fairy Wood, as the sound of singing came floating across the meadow and noticed the Fallow Deer arriving and called out across the meadow, "Bring your family over here Whitethorn, you are most welcome."

The singing became louder as, between two large oak trees, their leaf and acorn-laden branches forming a natural arch, stepped Herb-Robert, his Yew Fighting Staff held high.

All the animals from the Wild Wood fell silent and waited.

He strutted into the meadow and looked towards the waiting guests of his Queen, waived his greetings and turned and gestured to those waiting unseen behind him in the Fairy Wood.

The animals of the Wild Wood waived back.

Suddenly, through the arch came the Fairy gardeners pushing their laden wheelbarrows. They ran quickly up the path to the centre of the circle and began unloading Queen Celandine's fairy feast. First laying brightly coloured cloths down, as others arranged the food that clearly would feed all and all tastes, that afternoon. Another gardener took from his wheelbarrow large bottles of elderberry wine and cloudy Wild Wood beer, while those that would not touch the fermented elderberry or beer put their noses in the air and felt superior to those that would.

Grandad and the badger brothers licked their lips in delight as Gigi whispered in his ear "You can have two beakers of beer Grandad and not one more." She then smiled and kissed his cheek.

The Fairy Gardeners finished their unloading, collected their wheelbarrows and ran back into the wood as the singing grew louder.

Bobbin whispered to Titania, "Where's Queen Celandine's throne, the one she used at Yule?" she asked frowning.

"It's a picnic Bobbin, everyone sits on the grass at picnics," she answered smiling, "Look, here comes Queen Celandine!" and looked up at the clear blue sky, "It never rains at Litha".

From the arch of the two oaks, delicately stepping onto the pathway was Queen Celandine, holding hands with her two daughters Rhiannon and the younger Diana, who skipped along beside their mother smiling and singing.

"Aren't they beautiful," said Bobbin seeing the two children clearly for the first time, "they look just like their mother, don't you think?"

Gigi arrived and took Bobbin's hand and said, "Yes, they are and Rhiannon will make an excellent Queen when that time arrives, especially with Diana supporting her" and looked down at Bobbin and said seriously, "You should get to know them both" and kissed her cheek.

Bobbin frowned to herself, suspecting there was a hidden meaning in Gigi's last words and felt she needed to ask "Why?" but again something told her to wait and recalled both Grandad's and Lord Devon's words 'one of these days'.

Queen Celandine and her children stopped in front of Herb-Robert, who bowed deeply to the Queen and kissed her offered hand, then stepped forward and kissed both children on their cheeks, then turned and stepped out along the scythed path with his fighting stick raised, leading the Queen and her two princesses towards the circle and her cushions under the oak tree.

Behind their Queen emerged dozens of fairy children singing and waving small branches of summer leaves from trees in the Fairy Wood, with their mothers and fathers trying to keep the excited children on the path. Their fathers, waving horn beakers for the wine and beer, while their mothers, smiling and singing carried plates and napkins.

"What's the song they're singing Gigi?" Bobbin asked.

Gigi smiled and began to speak the words lyrically:

"Our hearts full of love and our arms open wide
We hold the keys to the fairy delight.
While the song in our hearts belongs in the air
The words of our wisdom we bring forth to share."

"Oh, Gigi the words are wonderful," said the enchanted Bobbin.

....

Queen Celandine reached her cushions and her children began to play with the other children. She looked about her, saw the Red Deer and walked over to them and formally greeted both Lord Devon and Lady Titania. From there, she spotted Whitethorn the Fallow Deer and quickly stepped over to him, giving his whole family her greetings and taking Whitethorn's head in her hands gently kissed his forehead and whispered in his ear.

Bobbin had been watching and wondering what the Queen had said to Whitethorn and looked over at Grandad and Gigi who were both smiling at her. Bobbin looked at her grand parents quizzically and asked, "What is it you two, what are you smiling for?" and they both shook their heads and continued smiling at her. She felt Manu brushing up against her leg and wagging his tail "What is it Manu?" she asked, but Manu just continued to wag his tail.

Oberon lowered his antlers and Reynard raised his brush tail in respect as Queen Celandine approached them. There she stopped and spoke quietly to them both, but Bobbin was too far away to hear her words and as she stepped away from them both. Oberon and Reynard glanced over at Bobbin and then quickly looked away.

Bobbin became even more puzzled and wondered what was going on, as the Queen greeted both Grandad and Gigi and finally turned to Bobbin and said, "Greetings my dear Bobbin, please come with me, I want you to meet my children" and took her hand and led her to the cushions under the oak. There, once seated the queen clapped her hands and a silence fell from those playing in the circle. The Queen called "Rhiannon, Diana please come and meet Miss Bobbin" and looked at her people and said, "and afterwards I want you all to come and meet our Miss Bobbin."

Bobbin looked over at Gigi, who raised her eyebrows and smiled in delight.

The two fairy children ran eagerly up to their mother and Bobbin and held out their hands to Bobbin for her to take.

Bobbin took their hands in hers and smiled at them both warmly and said quietly, "Hello Princess Rhiannon, hello Princess Diana I am so pleased to meet you both."

The princesses both curtseyed, "Oh, Miss Bobbin we have both wanted to meet you since we saw you at Yuletide" they both said together breathlessly, "and we hope to see you more often. Please visit us each time you come to the Wild Wood and please don't call us princesses. Let us be just like you and our mother and call each other by our given names" again they both spoke together, their voices as one.

"Wait behind the cushions please children, while our people come and greet Miss Bobbin," said Queen Celandine and waved to the waiting fairies.

The waiting fairies in one called out, "Hello Miss Bobbin, we are so very pleased to meet you" and began to sing as they approached:

"Greetings Miss Bobbin, will you come and stay
And dance in the cool sunlight all silver and sparkling bright.
Dancing in a little fairy ring, what magic will you bring.
Will you come and stay a while and let us go and play."

....

The fairy gardeners began distributing the food among their guests and all the animals and birds. There was a large bowl of food placed by the rabbits and smaller mice, different food for the badgers, weasels and stoats. For the Red Deer and the smaller Fallow Deer, they were given the succulent sweet grasses and wildflowers scythed that morning by the Fairy gardeners.

Larkspur the Weasel and Mouse Ear the Stoat crept up to the low branch of an oak that Alfred and Burnet were perched on. Burnet saw them and said "Uncle Alfred, we have visitors" and pointed with a wing tip to the Weasel and Stoat.

Alfred flapped his wings asking "What are you two doing here? You were not invited!"

Larkspur and Mouse Ear put their arms round each other, their eyes wide in fear of what might happen to them and each squeaked in turn "Alfred, Alfred please help us. We want to ask Lord Devon if he would allow us to live in the Wild Wood. It would make us so happy" both now breathless and fidgeting nervously.

Alfred thought for a moment, then making up his mind answered, "Well, you cannot just walk up the Lord Devon without being announced, let me think" and turned to Burnet and spoke quietly.

Burnet nodded his agreement and said to Larkspur and Mouse Ear, "You must speak to Miss Bobbin and ask her. She is the one now."

Both Larkspur and Mouse Ear looked at each other frowning and grinning in puzzlement, "What do you mean, she is 'the one'?"

Alfred responded impatiently, "Should you be invited to stay at the picnic you will find out. Go and speak with Miss Bobbin and do not step into the circle!" and flapped his wings irritably.

Bobbin was sat with Queen Celandine and Lady Titania, enjoying a bowl of salad and Fairy Bread. The Elderberry Wine and Cloudy Wild Wood Beer had been passed round to those that enjoyed the liquid. Grandad and Herb-Robert had joined the badger brothers and were waving their horn flasks and laughing. Gigi was surrounded by the squirrels, rabbits and birds all joyfully eating and speaking all at the same time.

Every now and then Gigi would look over at Grandad and give him a disapproving look, to which Grandad would raise his flask and smile. She would return his smile reluctantly for she loved seeing Grandad enjoying himself.

Hernshaw and Patience the Herons had joined Alfred and Burnet, the herons eating small fish caught by the Fairy Fishermen. While the two owls were enjoying their food that had been specially prepared by the Fairy Cooks and all happily chatting to each other.

Interestingly, Bobbin noticed Moonbeam the Otter was sitting with the ducks and their ducklings, quietly speaking to the older ducks and carefully playing with the ducklings and smiled to herself.

While Oberon and Reynard stood alert, either side of the Lord Devon, who from time to time looked at them both and smiled with pride.

Bobbin heard over the chatter and joyous singing two small voices calling her name. She looked over to where the voices came from and saw Larkspur and Mouse Ear standing at the edge of the circle, calling and waving at her and turned to the Fairy Queen "Celandine, would you excuse me? I am wanted over there" and pointed.

"Of course, my child" Celandine replied, "But please come back soon, for we have much to discuss before the dancing begins."

"I will," Bobbin said as she stood up frowning to herself again, being reminded of the curious words of Grandad and Gigi, then by Alfred. She shook her head, puzzled and walked over the edge of the fairy ring.

"Hello, you two," she greeted Larkspur and Mouse Ear, "What can I do for you?" she asked smiling happily at them both.

Bobbin's greeting and disarming smile put them both at ease, especially as they had seen Lord Devon's disapproving gaze at them before Bobbin arrived.

"Miss Bobbin," said Larkspur and Mouse Ear, "would you take us over to Lord Devon please" and stopped and grinned nervously as Larkspur spoke "We want to ask the Lord Devon if we can live in the Wild Wood forever" and both of them took each other in his arms and looked from Bobbin to Lord Devon a number of times.

"Let me ask the Queen's permission first," said Bobbin seriously, "It is the fairies' day of celebration."

"Of course, Miss Bobbin, of course" and looked again nervously over at the Lord Devon.

"Celandine, may I leave the circle and take Larkspur and Mouse Ear to Lord Devon?" she asked.

"Yes my dear, let me have Herb-Robert take you from the circle" and looked over and saw her consort singing and carousing with Grandad and the badger brothers, Cloudy Wild Wood Beer slopping from a flask held precariously in his waving hand, his coat of Forest Green discarded, his shirt unbuttoned, his fighting pole, cudgel and belt strewn on the grass beside his forsaken hat.

The Fairy Queen looked at Bobbin and giggled "Look at them over there" and laughed with delight, happily knowing they were enjoying themselves. "Come with me my child and I will escort you and see what my dear Herb-Robert does" and laughed again.

The Fairy Queen stood and took Bobbin's hand. Immediately Herb-Robert noticed and watched. The Queen giggled again and grinned at Bobbin, "Let us walk to the edge of the circle" and giggled once more.

Herb-Robert gathered himself, putting down his horn flask and strode purposely towards his Queen.

Queen Celandine giggled again as Herb-Robert's steps became awkward, he staggered once and managed to remain upright, then at the edge of the circle he finally fell flat on his face and the Queen began rocking with laughter and clung to Bobbin in delight.

Bobbin began laughing herself, not at Herb-Robert, but the Queen's infectious laughter as she said between her laughs and giggles, "My dearest Herb-Robert amuses me at every Litha celebration, once he joins with Grandad, Bardon and Blade. Isn't he just wonderful" and winked at Bobbin and called to her consort "Herb-Robert my dear, you should take yourself back to your drinking companions, Miss Bobbin will take care of us" she said in mild disapproval.

At the edge of the circle the Queen stopped, kissed Bobbin's cheek and said "Off you go my child. Don't be long, I shall miss you."

"Come on you two," said Bobbin politely to Larkspur and Mouse Ear, "Let's go and see Lord Devon."

Larkspur and Mouse Ear looking nervously and wide-eyed took each other's hand and followed Bobbin.

On reaching the Lord Devon, Bobbin stopped and waited respectfully for the Red Deer to notice her.

Lord Devon finished speaking with Alfred and Talon the Crow from the High Moor, as his nephew Meadow Crow-Foot and Burnet waited behind them. "So my friend Talon, it is agreed. Please eat and enjoy yourself, I will announce our agreement shortly" and looked over and saw Bobbin waiting.

"Miss Bobbin," called the Red Deer, "you wish to speak with me?"

"Yes Lord Devon," said Bobbin and hesitated for a moment, thinking and then took a breath, "I ask you to speak with Larkspur the Weasel and Mouse Ear the Stoat. They have a request."

The Red Deer looked down on the weasel and stoat, shook his antlers once and said "Speak."

Larkspur and Mouse Ear clung to each other for courage and began to babble their request.

Lord Devon looked at Bobbin and said kindly, "I think they need your help Miss Bobbin."

"Yes we do, we do Miss Bobbin," gasped Larkspur and Mouse Ear together.

Bobbin smiled and nodded at Lord Devon, "They are asking to be able to make their home in the Wild Wood for ever, my Lord," she said courteously.

Alfred heard Bobbin's request and flew to Lord Devon and whispered in his ear.

Lord Devon nodded to Alfred and smiled at Bobbin "I am of a mind to grant their request Miss Bobbin" and looked over at the Weasel and Stoat, "Perhaps you will be of use to the folk hereabouts and from time-to-time, Alfred will have a task for you both. Welcome to the Wild Wood."

Both Larkspur and Mouse Ear screamed their delight and ran round in circles and danced off and joined the other Weasels and Stoats.

Bobbin thanked Lord Devon and he responded with "No Miss Bobbin, I thank you, for we will use both Larkspur and Mouse Ear as our eyes and ears the next time those dreadful rogue Foxes and Rats from the mountains beyond the High Moor threaten us" and looked down at her and said, "I am making Talon and his nephew Meadow Crow-Foot our Ambassadors at Large on the High Moor. For parts of the moorland can be neglected in the wintertime. They both will be most helpful to us. Don't you think Miss Bobbin? Talon is most clever and will be able to train young Meadow Crow-Foot for the future."

Bobbin again frowned, thinking what Lord Devon could have meant by 'the future' but nodded her agreement knowing it was about time she spoke with Grandad and Gigi seriously.

"Thank you Lord Devon," said Bobbin and nodded to Alfred, "May I return to Queen Celandine?"

"There is a need for some more of your time Miss Bobbin. Would you step with us to the edge of the circle?" and the Red Deer stepped forward with Lady Titania, followed by Oberon their son, Alfred his councillor, Reynard and the two badger brothers.

Bobbin's curiosity deepened, as Grandad and Gigi joined her and together they walked to the edge of the circle and saw that Whitethorn the Fallow Deer had joined Lord Devon.

175

Queen Celandine was waiting for them and asked Bobbin to stand with her, as the Lord of the Wild Wood, the Oak Wood where the Fairies lived and the High Moor stepped forward and raised his head and spoke:

"A happy Litha to you all my dear friends. A special greeting to you your Majesty and all your people" and lowered his head and gently shook his antlers, then raised his head and said, "I have two announcements firstly, my Lady Titiania is with child!"

There was an immediate cheering by all gathered in the meadow, with the fairies clapping and dancing in their circle, with squeaks of excitement from the birds in the trees and the animals on the ground.

Lord Devon raised his head and shook his antlers once and the meadow fell silent. "My trusted friend Reynard the Fox will become guardian to our child, to watch over in the daylight and the darkness" and looked over at Titania.

Reynard stood in stunned silence, his nose even higher in the air and his friend Oberon whispered to him, "Your nose is now too high in the air, much too high you silly fox." Reynard did not hear him, he was in a world of his own importance.

Lord Devon stood quietly for several moments and allowed his people to settle and then continued, "Secondly, I have given permission for Larkspur and Mouse Ear to live in the Wild Wood, they will be of use to us and I ask you to welcome them."

Bobbin looked round and saw Larkspur and Mouse Ear dancing in circles with the other Stoats and Weasels.

"And finally, my friend Whitethorn has a request and will speak with our Miss Bobbin," announced the Red Deer.

Queen Celandine then took Bobbin's hand and gave her a reassuring smile as Whitethorn the Fallow Deer waited next to Lord Devon.

"Miss Bobbin," said Lord Devon, and all the fairies in the circle drew nearer and all the animals and birds of the Wild Wood at the edge of the circle listened, "Whitethorn of the Fallow Deer has a request. Would you hear him?"

A sudden calm swept over Bobbin, as Queen Celandine let go of her hand and allowed her to step closer to the Fallow Deer, as all her uncertainty and confusion faded away. She smiled at Whitethorn as she began to repeat the words of the tiny voice inside her head, "Hello again Whitethorn, I am so very pleased to speak with you once more and happy to hear your request" and placed her hand on Whitethorn's shoulder and looked up at Alfred.

Alfred nodded reassuringly and flapped his wings twice.

"Miss Bobbin," said Whitethorn, and lowered his head for a moment then raised it once more saying quietly, "I ask that my tribe and I be allowed to live in the Wild Wood and make our home here" and lowered his head again respectfully.

The surprised Bobbin looked at Grandad and Gigi, who both smiled at her and nodded their heads and Grandad said quietly, "There is enough of the woodland for them and they will be good for the wood. We'll put them close to our cottage and they'll have the grasses and wildflowers of Misty Meadow to feed on. But you must give Whitethorn your permission formally."

Bobbin not quite over her surprise was about to ask *"Why me?"* when the little voice in her head told her not to, and turned back and faced Whitethorn repeating the words that came into her head. "You and your tribe are most welcome my dear Whitethorn. Please speak with my Great Grandfather and he will show you where you will be most comfortable."

There was a delighted and excited cry that came from the Fallow Deer herd, "Thank you Miss Bobbin, thank you."

Whitethorn raised his head high and shook his antlers twice and said, "I thank you Miss Bobbin and look forward to seeing you often and introducing you to my family and tribe."

....

The Fairy Queen stood up from her cushions and her fairy people fell silent. She raised her arms and called "Let us dance" and the singing started again, this time with the haunting sound of Pan Pipes being played by three of the fairy children and the dancing began as the fairies all joined together in a large ring and began to dance round the edges of the circle.

All the other animals and birds watched this spectacular and strangely haunting scene for a few moments, then all came together and danced themselves in the opposite direction to the fairies, round the outer edges of the fairy ring in the bright afternoon sunlight.

Bobbin returned to Queen Celandine and settled herself on the cushions as Lord Devon and Lady Titania arrived followed shortly after by Grandad and Gigi.

The Queen stood up and held her hands out to Bobbin and gently pulled her up. Bobbin was intrigued and did not speak but noticed Alfred arriving and settling himself on a low branch of the oak. All the others were smiling at her as Celandine spoke, "Bobbin our dearest child, we welcome you to our council of which one day soon we will ask you to take Grandad's place and take care of us all in the Wild Wood, The Fairy Wood and the High Moor as Grandad and Gigi has done for so long" and looked at Lord Devon who shook his great antlers twice and said, "You would do us great honour to except this Miss Bobbin and give us great confidence for all our futures here in this heavenly countryside.

Bobbin was completely taken aback and gasped her surprise as the words Wild Wood, Fairy Wood and the High Moor echoed through her head and spoke her thoughts carefully:

"You do me a great honour, you really do" and looked at each of her friends and Grandad and Gigi, "But I am too young and inexperienced for such a responsibility, why can't Grandad and Gigi carry on?"

It was Alfred who answered her question, "They will of course Miss Bobbin and give you time to finish your education and learn all the things you will need to know. But having all spoken amongst ourselves we of the Wild Wood, the Fairy Wood and the High Moor need you to secure our lives in the future."

"But the Wild Wood and the Fairy Wood and the High Moor must first of all be secured from people who would clear the trees to build more and more houses" and she felt the tears begin to run down her cheeks and quickly wiped them away, "Who owns this land of ours?" she cried, as more tears began to flow down her cheeks.

Grandad and Gigi came to her side and put their arms around her as Queen Celandine, Lord Devon, Titania and Alfred came closer and Grandad spoke, "You do, our dearest Bobbin, you do."